Just Like in

Light, ~~camera~~ , reaction

Just Like in the Movies

Light, ~~camera~~, reaction

Rahul Saini

Srishti
PUBLISHERS & DISTRIBUTORS

SRISHTI PUBLISHERS & DISTRIBUTORS
N-16, C. R. Park
New Delhi 110 019
srishtipublishers@gmail.com

First published by Srishti Publishers & Distributors in 2010
Third impression 2011
Copyright © Rahul Saini, 2010

This is entirely a work of fiction. All characters and events are totally imaginary.

Typeset in AGaramond 11pt. by Suresh Kumar Sharma at Srishti

Printed and bound in India

"Success is not money or power; success is waking up in the morning, so excited about what you have to do, that you literally fly out the door."

— Jenny Garrison, Fame (2009)

"Don't tell me not to live, just sit and putter
Life's candy and the sun's a ball of butter
Don't bring around a cloud to rain on my parade..."

— *Funny Girl (1968)*

How it all began...

If you are wondering how it happened – and what it is all about this time, let me start by saying that I conceived a major part of this story while watching the evening re-runs of the auditions for *Dance India Dance*. I had been advised to stay at home and rest in order to regain my strength and stamina, fully recover from the recent bouts of illnesses. So every evening I would sit down to watch that show and find myself literally weeping at the end of each episode. The emotion that emerged seeing all those contestants coming from far-flung corners of our country with so much hope, determination, faith, and most of all, courage was really strong.

Watching the show, I realized two things – we in India, have talented dancers of truly international caliber. But, I saw so many people plainly mesmerized by the glamour of the entertainment industry. They were completely carried away by it in believing that they could also have a career here when they didn't in actuality possess any talent.

Another issue that I have tried to touch in this story is the capriciousness of 'romantic relationships' that our youth seem to indulge in. I am not saying that there is anything wrong in that, or that they should be frowned upon, but I would like the youth to know that such relationships are a part of their journeys to self-discovery, and they should be aware of their actions.

Thirdly, how can anyone write a story in these times without talking about the terrible *recession* that is affecting us in every sphere? And I have to admit that it was fun watching my characters' reactions when they were first hit by it.

And lastly, like most of my stories, this one is also about following your heart, learning how to listen to its voice and achieving your dreams. Well, I guess this is all you guys need before you start the story. I hope you all have as much fun reading the story, as I had writing it.

Cheers!

Rahul Saini

August 20, 2009

On a humid, sunny afternoon (with rain clouds visible at a distance.)

Part One

Amit – The one who starts with saying that his life sucks (almost always)

I have seen *Rock On*. AND I KNOW HOW IT'S GOING TO BE IN A COUPLE OF YEARS! I will wake up every morning and with robotic precision, get ready and push off to work. IT'S FREAKY!!!!

Yes, it's as simple as that. And I think it's time to accept the fact that my job sucks and so does my life. Right now, I really can't see a single thing that is going right. Sehar, my girlfriend says that it's very human to feel this way. She is a psychologist, she should know. She gifted me a book yesterday – *Eat Pray Love*. It has Julia Roberts on the cover saying – "*This is what I am giving all my girlfriends.*" I wonder what Sehar has up her sleeve at times. It almost surprises me like a magician's act.

I seriously do not understand why we choose the lives we live. I mean why did I leave my beautiful hometown of Dehradun and come all the way here? TO GURGAON! TO LIVE ALL ALONE!!! When it is so very tough this way! You have to manage your own food, laundry… and worst of all – FINANCES! As it is, earning money is not so simple. Then, to top it all – it's even more difficult to manage it! File your returns, pay taxes!!! Can you beat that?

AND YOU EVEN HAVE TO CLEAN YOUR OWN ROOM!!! Good God! Just look at my room, I feel like I live in a garbage dump. Mounds of clothes and empty packets of wafers all around, I have not even found the space to empty the bag I brought back from my last visit home! That was two and a half weeks ago.

OH NO! Its 1:30 AM! I must go to sleep or I will be late for office tomorrow! It's already tomorrow! I would love to get up sick, just not in any condition to report to work. But before I crash, I must jot down my to-do list.

— Clean the room
— Unpack the bag
— Separate the washed clothes from the dirty ones
— Buy fruits (find out what apples cost these days. ask mom.)
— Join gym (by all means)
— Hire a maid to cook and clean
— Save up for the ipod.

Rishika – The one who does not say too much (or does she?)

Frantically, I get out of the car and run up the stairs – flat number 28 – B. With all my might I bang on the door repeatedly.

"AMIT, GET UP! WE ARE GOING TO BE LATE FOR OFFICE!"

I wait for seven seconds and bang on the door again "AMIT! GET UP!!!!!"

Sleepy-eyed and yawning lazily Amit opens the door, rubbing his eyes while his hair falls across his face.

"O God! You are so useless! And when the hell are you going to learn how to drive? I am sick of driving you around."

"Sorry" he says scratching his head, frowning and looking confused simultaneously.

"And why the hell don't you pick up your phone?"

"Were you calling?" he asks picking up the phone from the table next to his bed, "Oh! It died again. Now I *need* a new phone," he says, punching a few keys when the front panel of the phone detaches itself from the rest of it and falls on the floor.

I put the panel back on the table and say, "Yes, I guessed that, when I called you in the morning to wake you up. That is why I rushed here early. I knew that since the phone was not working, there would be no wake up alarm for you this morning. Now, would you please hurry up and get ready? And just look at the place! It's like you are living in a trash can! You need a girlfriend."

"Madam, you forget. I *have* a girlfriend."

"Huh! I meant a real girlfriend. Not an ex – counselor – from – your – previous – office – who – had – a – crush – on – you kind-of-a girlfriend. God! I remember how she used to hit on you. All those low neck lines and all that cleavage."

"Come on, you know that is not true. She never hit on me. I fell for her." Amit says.

"Really Amit?"

"Really Rishi."

"Really Amit?"

"Rishi, we are getting late."

Amit – he dislikes his office (but then, who doesn't?)

"See you in the evening." I say as I hop out of the car in front of the glass building. It almost hurts my eye to look at the sunrays bouncing off the façade.

"Yes. Bye." Rishika says as she steps on the accelerator.

Holding my laptop bag, and most uncomfortably dressed in formals, I walk on the polished marble floor of the corridor to my office

"Hi Harry, Hi Manu, Hi Ajay, …" I greet everyone as I walk to my workstation.

I settle down in my seat, switch on my computer, look fondly at the flowers Sehar had sent me the day before. My head tilts to one side involuntarily as I lose myself in thoughts about her.

"Morning Amit"

"Morning … Ma'am," I fumble. It is my team leader Shobha standing in front of me.

"The meeting is in ten minutes in the conference room. See you there. And call me Shob. How many times do I need to tell you that" she says as she walks away.

"… Yes… sure ma'am... Shob…" I stammer.

The conference room is tidily set for the meeting. All the senior members of the firm troop in, in a single file and take their seats. Within three minutes the room is full and everyone is hurriedly going through the notebooks and folders.

I carefully, and most responsibly, unroll the map of Gurgaon, which is the subject of discussion today. The Director of the firm enters the room with brisk and energetic stride and everyone stands to attention.

He stops at one end of the table, nods, and sits down. The sound of silk ruffling against chairs echoes in the room. My cheap cotton pants, of course make the least amount of noise.

"As we all know, we are here to talk about the new township that we are going to develop. It would be an extension of our existing township here," the Director points at a spot on the map on the periphery of Gurgaon. Everyone nods with blind, thoughtless approval. I feel a sudden punch of shock. That land is …

"But sir, this land… it is the essential grazing ground for cattle and is owned by villagers of the neighboring village."

And not only that! That is the place Rishi, Rima and I go picnic every month!!!

The room falls silent. I look around, but no one meets my gaze. Suddenly the director starts laughing loudly. And everyone else in the room follows his cue including Shobha who looks at me, frowning as she laughs. "Amit; real estate, is what we do. Are you forgetting that?" the director says as everyone instantly switches to a serious expression again.

"No sir… I mean that … as planners … we should think of the ecology and the…"

"Yes, yes; I know you are fresh out of college. Shob, do I need to train *you* again or …"

"No, no sir, ha ha ha" she delivers a pretentious, carefree laugh as she throws her head back. "You don't have to worry. I will train him. I know how to." she says as she gives me a look la Meryl Streep from *The Devil Wears Prada* (She may have imagined herself as such, but to me, she looks just like an angry goat. All that is missing are a pair of long ears but her outlandish earrings more than make up for that.)

"So, as I was saying, this township would be one of a kind, luxury township in all of India, with the most lavish golf courses, malls and multiplexes. It would be an attraction for all the rich and famous – a weekend home. We would promote it thus '*A peaceful home away from home.*' What do you think?"

Everyone applauds.

'Wow! Great idea."

"I love the line sir, – a home away from home. I think it will click."

"Superb!"

"Mind-blowing sir, mind blowing I can tell you."

It is disgusting to see them - shameless sycophants.

So the meeting goes on. For some twenty minutes or more. After that, we all go to our respective workstations to carry out the day's work. It is about an hour later that Shobha comes to me and says,

"Amit, do you like your job?"

NO! I DON'T! I HATE IT! WHAT WE DO HERE IS DOWNRIGHT IMMORAL! MAKING THOSE NON-REQUIRED FANCY TOWNSHIPS FOR SOME STINKING RICH PEOPLE WHO WANT ONE-MORE-HOUSE AWAY FROM THE HUSTLE BUSTLE OF THE CITY AND STARVING THE POOR VILLAGERS!!!! This is what I want to say, but what I say, or rather stammer is –

"…No ma'am… I mean, yes ma'am …Shob." Oh! How I hate calling her that. She is such a wanna be!

"No, or yes Amit?" she glares at me.

"I mean, yes, I like my job. In fact I *love* my job."

"Good, then you sure wouldn't like to lose it. Would you?"

"Yes, … I mean no. Never… Shob."

"Good. Then be more careful in the meetings."

"Yes ma'am. Shob."

"Good. And has the proposal for the land-use pattern come from the consultants?"

"Yes, yes it has."

"Good. Get a printout of that, I want to see it. I will be waiting in my cabin." With that she walks away, her high-heeled leather shoes, deliberately making that tap-tap sound on the floor.

Rishika – Some people have it all. (Or so it appears)

I know I am late for office by a good twenty minutes, but there is a way to handle everything. I confidently walk out of the office parking lot and put on an expression that is essentially a mixture of composure and seriousness and walk into my office building. Entering my cabin, I switch on my laptop and drum my fingers on the table as I wait for the machine to boot. I look at the watch – 10:30 AM. Only an hour left for the meeting. My presentation on market response and 'suggestion set' for the new soap launched by a client firm is going to be under the scanner today.

A deep breath later, I set down to work.

At 11:30 AM I am ready with my opening remarks.

Pointing at the image of the graph the projector is projecting on the screen, I say.

"As you can see the sales have risen following the last promotional campaign. It is true that even in today's world most of us Indians do desire fair skin." I pause deliberately taking in the guilty looks on the faces in the audience.

"My suggestion is that we take this campaign forward and maybe hire a top Bollywood star for our next campaign. I welcome all suggestions." I smile and look at all the people sitting around the table.

"Sounds good." Mr. Arun Kumar finally speaks up. "I would love to have Kareena Kapoor for the campaign. She is my son's hot favorite!" he says as he chuckles. "After all it's a great way to cash in on her whole 'size zero' publicity. Deepika works too. She is *my* favorite."

"But isn't she… like very … dusky and not *fair*?" a hesitant voice queries.

"Oh! Make up takes care of it all. That is just not a problem." says another voice. "Well, I would say Deepika is a good option."

The chitchat continues for a good ten minutes and finally the meeting ends.

"Good job Rish."

I turn around with a confident smile to meet the Director, Arun Kumar.

"Thank you Arun."

"At times I really wonder how you manage all this. Your personal and your professional life, so adequately balanced."

"It's not all that tough. It's just that we need to think a little less about it, at times. Everything falls right into place by itself."

"Ha ha ha! I love it. Always ready with humor. Good."

I force an awkward smile on my face. I am I was serious about it.

"Good. See you at lunch." He says as he leaves.

Amit – And some people don't have anything.

Work or no work, deadline or no deadline, I am leaving the office today at six. I look at my watch, its 5:55 P.M

"Amit have you prepared the minutes of the morning meeting?" Shobha leans back, rolls her chair a little so she can see me as she peeps out of her cabin.

"Yes ma'am. No ma'am, … I mean I'll just get it in… ten minutes."

She rolls her eyes with an expression of disappointment and goes back to her cabin. Ok, so what, just ten minutes lost! I will still be able to leave the office at six-ten instead of a neat six. That is not a big deal, right?

After exactly seven minutes I get up from my chair to hand over the minutes of the meeting to Shob.

"Hmm," she looks at it critically as if it is a legal divorce application filed by her husband and not simple minutes of a meeting.

"Ok, so have you prepared the presentation that I am supposed to deliver for tomorrow's meeting?"

"…Aaaah, not yet ma'am… I mean Shob" What is she talking about? Isn't she supposed to prepare that herself?

"Ok. Do that quickly. And please let me have that presentation within the hour. I need to go through it before I leave."

"Yes Shob."

Another day's six-ten fantasy meets a tragic end!

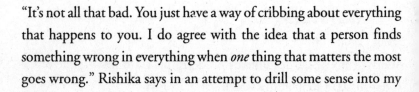

"It's not all that bad. You just have a way of cribbing about everything that happens to you. I do agree with the idea that a person finds something wrong in everything when *one* thing that matters the most goes wrong." Rishika says in an attempt to drill some sense into my head.

"… That sounded a little …complex." I say.

She gives me one of her typical how-dumb-could-you-get-in-life look. I quickly try to run the words she has just uttered back in my head.

"Hmm, it does make a little sense."

"Not little, *all*. It makes *all the sense*. And it's just an *office*, Amit; I don't understand why you don't take it the way it should be taken. You just need to go and work to simply earn a living. *Without* getting too involved in it. And what you should get more involved in is your personal life, which, you don't seem to be getting much involved in at all. I don't like repeating myself, but you really need a better girlfriend. Not a girlfriend who clings to you just for show."

I sit there as she drones on fully engrossed and wide eyed just like people we have seen on TV listening to one of Baba Ram Dev's lectures when I feel something vibrating madly in the pocket of my jeans. I quickly whip out my phone......It is Sehar.

"Hey! Hi! Don't tell me you are going to be late again." I say. This is a daily thing with Sehar. She is always late for all our meetings.

"Actually honey, I won't be able to make it today. One of my patients is really upset and I am planning an extra session with him."

"Oh, ok. Hmm. *Chalo,* you take care. See you tomorrow then."

"Byeeeeee" she says.

"Bye" I say, smiling, pleased at her chirpiness.

I look up and see Rishika has already opened her mouth to say something.

"Don't!" I butt in; "Everyone is not as lucky as you to find a perfect partner for life."

She reclines on the chair quietly. "So Iman's left for Bangalore?"

"Yes." she says.

Who is Iman? He is Rishika's boyfriend. They have been going around officially for three long years. Sure, some people are capable of making a relationship work this long today.

"And when is Rimz returning?" I ask.

"Tomorrow."

"Thank God! I really need some energy back in my life."

Rimz – The material girl.

Grooving to the beats of the song (Madonna's *Material Girl*) playing on her computer, she looks around for her new hexagonal metal bangles. "Oh, here they are!" she says with a cheerful smile as she turns around like a film star with her hair gracefully billowing in the air. She is dressed in an attractive black and white outfit that fits her like second skin. "And there you are!" she says as she greets us with a warm and welcoming smile. "Thank you so much dear narrator, you are such a darling. Thank you so much for this on-request-film star-like-intro. I can take it from here on. You can take a break now. Go on! Have a Coke or something."

Hi! I am Rimz… as you can see I am getting ready for office. In fact I am almost done. And I am about to leave. I will tell you something about myself on the way to work. It's such a dull ride everyday! Anyway, what was I saying? Oh yes, the office. If you really ask me, I don't think that I am meant for this job. I mean, I'm not meant for *arranging* star-studded events. I am meant to be a star *for* such events. But if you really ask me *right now*, I don't mind. I get to interact with all the stars, I manage the biggest events in the city, get invites for all the major fashion shows. Actually, I kind of like it. The best part is, at the end of the month, *I get money*. I shop till I drop and for my shopping, well, the scene is not as exciting as it should be. My calculations are pretty simple though – I get Rupees 70 K per month. In the best possible situation, I should be buying 4 dresses, worth Rupees 20 K each. But sadly that does not happen. Rupees 20 K goes to pay the rent and meet the food expenses. Another 20 goes into entertainment. You know, movies, discos and all. Some 10K is allocated to meeting unforeseen expenses, the sorts we normally have: bad hair days and hair related disasters ranking at the very top there. So I am left with only Rupees 20 K which means an average of one dress a month, unless there is a sale on. The best four letter word there is, *sale*, to me means, I can splurge. But otherwise I live like a pauper. But it's not all *that* bad. Oh! We are here. See that's my office building, over there, that one with the shiny glass facade. I have to go now and do some *work*. I will catch you later. Take care. Bye bye☺

I can't believe they started the book without me! Anyway, it's ok. I am going to rule the book and I know it.)

Ugh! It's so irritating coming back to office after a nice long vacation. Europe was so much fun. The feel of the Tuscan sun is still so fresh in my mind. I wish my Dad would gift me another such trip. Hmm. Anyway.

"Hi Rima, how was the trip?"

I turn around, it is Vinnie. For a second I forget his question, and I lose myself in his eyes. O God! They are so divine. He is the most devastatingly handsome guy in our office. Secretly, we all call him the Greek God. He is tall, fair, with broad shoulders and an athletic build. Hmm. He says he is single but I am sure he has a girlfriend tucked away someplace. He just doesn't like talking about her. It is a very personal matter for some people, after all. *And* deep down he is a very shy person. I know that. But that's ok, I plan to find out about her, split them up, and keep him all for myself. And then, we will go live in a valley somewhere, next to a river, in a castle with...

"Rima? What happened?"

"Oh Yeah!" Oh no! What is he talking about? What is he saying? AH! I remember! "Yes, the trip, it was very nice. It was all *so* beautiful. I just wanted to settle there in some valley, by a river, in a castle." I say looking into his eyes

"I am sure you will one day" he says with a laugh, flashing his perfect pearly whites.

"See you around." he walks away quite the model on the ramp.

"Rima. Hi!"

"Huh?" It is Deepika, my immediate boss. And she is a darling. I have never seen a better boss. Although this is my first job, but I can sense it like everyone else that she is so understanding.

"Oh hi! Morning" I say

"Morning. So how was the trip?" she asks

"Oh it was good. Could not have been better. Did loads and loads of shopping. From Gucci to Prada to Chanel to everything." How nice it feels when people ask you how 'did your wonderful trip go?'

"Good to know that. See you around."

Hmm.... it seems that there is no major event happening these days, as no one seems to be talking about any work. I go to my workstation, put my expensive Gucci bag on the table and switch on my computer.

"Hi Rima! Back? How was the trip?"

Uh! Now it's not all that fun when everyone asks you the same

16

question *over and over* again you know! This is Pooja by the way. I am not her fan. She's the one with the worst fashion sense imaginable. And she always insists that I keep my bag in that little storage space provided in our workstation unit. I don't have a cheap and ugly bag like she does, you know. I can't keep mine in that tiny little slit that they provide. Today, however, seems to be an exception – she hasn't mentioned it yet.

"Nice bag. Is it new?"

"Yes, I bought it from London."

"Wow! You know next time you go, would you get one for me as well? We don't get such nice stuff in Delhi."

Why? So you can put it in that tiny little slit in your workstation to completely destroy its shape? "Yeah, Sure." I smile.

"*Vasay* you should put the bag on that shelf there, or you are going to get a mail from the HR department to un-clutter your desk." Ah! Here it comes again.

"Oh! That." I say throwing my head back as I let out a tiny laugh "I couldn't care less, about the mails."

She passes me a stupid smile, which seems to have some message in it but I am just not interested in decoding it.

Amit – Its time (for you) to meet his girlfriend.

I sit waiting at CCD occupying a tiny little chair with a table. Someone is already sitting at the table with the couch. How I hate it when that happens. But it's ok. I have asked one of the friendly ever smiling waiters to serve the people sitting there quickly so that they finish their coffee and leave swiftly. I can then, move into that vacant corner. Sehar and I are supposed to meet at 7 PM here. I think she is on schedule. Its 7:25, and according to her record, she should be here by 7:30. I sit there browsing the latest issue of *Time Out*, looking for any interesting play that we could go for over the weekend. I am almost through with my lemon-iced tea when the waiter informs me that I can shift to the other table. I get up, pick my bag and my coat when I notice Sehar coming in and walking towards me with brisk steps." I am so sorry. The traffic was mad today. It just wouldn't… move."

"It's ok." I say with a smile. How pretty she looks in that dress. Just like a doll. She reminds me of Keira Knightley, the way she looked in *Love Actually*.

"How's your patient?" I ask her as we sit down.

"Huh? Which patient?" she asks confused.

"The client? The one who kept you up yesterday? So you could not come."

"Oh *that* patient! He is ok. He is doing good. Actually he and his wife are having a case of inter-role conflict."

"Inter-role conflict?" I ask confused. It's really amazing how much knowledge she has stored in that tiny little head of hers. I mean I don't seem to hold even half of that in mine.

"Yes, it's a case we study in gender psychology. It's when a man's gender-role is fulfilled by a woman and woman's by a man. But it's going to work out. It's going to be just fine. I am sure of that. It's just going to take time but they will be fine"

Hmm. It sounds a little……… but its ok. She is the psychologist, and I am not, so I don't really need to probe deeper.

"Hmm. What's his name?" I ask.

"His name… what's his name…" she tries to recall when her phone starts to ring. "Oh! Look we were talking about him and he is calling." She says as she takes the call.

I look at her admiringly as she talks very professionally to her patient "Hello… yes… ok… ok… yes. Don't worry honey I will be right there." She says as she hangs up.

"Sorry sweets but I have to go."

"What? But we have not even had coffee yet."

"Sorry hon, I need to rush. He just had a fight with her and he is *very* upset."

"Ok…, but why do you work so hard?"

"Satisfaction darling, it satisfies me." As she says said this she looks deep in thought and then says, "I've got to rush now."

"Wait! Can we go for a play this weekend?" I shout behind her.

"Yeah. Sure, see you later. Bye."

I slump on the couch and wave the waiter for the bill.

Amit – when old friends reunite after ages (after …3 months actually)

I enter the restaurant and I can hear Rima saying "Amit can never make it on time. He and Sehar are so made for each other." They have just seen me enter the restaurant and I am late by thirty minutes.

"Oh! Here he is." Rishi says as she notices me coming towards the table.

"*Ok.* Look who is *back.*" It's so nice to meet your old friends after what? A month? But we are used to seeing each other every day.

I sit down and pick up the menu. We are having dinner at the Golden Dragon. We all happen to love Chinese.

"So have we ordered anything?" Knowing very well that neither of them would have ordered anything, I say "Let's start with some appetizers."

"Amit, do you realize if you keep eating like this you are soon going to develop a paunch?" Rishika says.

"Nope. I am going to join a gym this week. So, I am not going to develop a paunch, *in fact*, I am going to develop the abs."

"Yes, yes, we have been listening to this for over a year now."

"Yes, and now it's time to just do it!"

"You know something," Rima says as she looks at me, "you would *so* love London! It is the best place for foodies. Such a wide variety of food. So many cuisines! You won't believe it. There was this one restaurant that just served dim sums. I mean momos. And so many different kinds of momos. It was really good. But *very* expensive." She says as her expression turns serious.

"Yes, so momos is what we will start with." I say brightly. God! I just cannot wait. My mouth is already watering.

"So, anything big happening at work?" Rishi asks Rima.

"Nah, not really. Things have gone slow. It's because of the recession they say. People are hardly having any events or parties these days." Rima says

"Hmm, I might be arranging one soon. It's for that fairness soap I mentioned." Rishi says.

"Soup? Anyone?" I ask.

"Not for me." Rima

"Me neither." Rishi.

"Okay, one hot and sour veg. soup, one plate dim sums, and…?" I look around trying to figure out if anyone wants to suggest starters. "Nothing. Hey Amit, what project are you working on?"

"Me? Oh yes! On the project of the demolition of the greens where we had the picnic last time, Remember? On the way to Sohna?"

"Oh no! They are building there as well?" they both chorus.

"Yes!" I say as I skim the menu card. We have still not decided what we are going to have for the main course.

"Amit, you must do something!" Rishi says totally alarmed.

"Yes, and that is why I am going through this. And you should also pick one and decide." There is seldom any point in arguing with Rishi and this seems the best time to change the topic.

"Not this you idiot!" she says snatching the menu card as I sit there making faces and shrugging my shoulders.

"Hmm, yes, good idea, Why don't you come over some day and try reasoning with Shob *or* the director for that matter?" I say.

"It's your job, not mine. And believe me, if I did, they would change their minds." Rishi says

"Yes, yes" I reply.

"Any way, I don't need to get into this. As it is I have a million problems of my own." Rishi says.

"Oh! That reminds me! How are things with Iman? Are you going to tell your parents?"

"I think I will have to do that sooner than I thought *yaar*. They are really getting freaked out about my marriage! They have created accounts on every matrimonial website there is. Even on the ones that I had never heard of. Did you know there is a site called getmate.com? Anyway, I am going to meet a guy tomorrow. God, it feels so … sick! I mean when I know who I am going to marry, then why do I need to meet these people and pretend? *It's almost like I am cheating on Iman.* I think, I will talk to my parents tomorrow after meeting this guy,"

"Hmm" Rima says.

"Really! Are you sure you are ready to get married?" I ask

"Huh!" she sighs. "Well I have been listening to my parents for a very long time now. When am I going to get married? When will I have children? It's tough to raise kids after you hit 40. I think I will get married, if not today, then, someday. So, why not get it over with and get one thing out of the way?"

Good God! Are we that old that we need to start thinking when we are going to have *children*? I think we are children ourselves! How can children raise children? God! It's ridiculous to even imagine!

"Anyway, that is something that is going to take its own course. You tell me Rima, how are things going with Vinnie?" Rishi says

"Oh! Good. Things are good with him. It's just that he is very shy. I think I am going to have to make the first move. God, he is so delicious!"

"Great! So are we ordering now?" Are these people even interested in eating? I AM STARVING HERE!!!!! "Yes Amit, yes. *Chal* Rima lets order first, or Amit's going to have our brains for dinner."

Rimz – She is in love ;)

"But why didn't you tell me if you liked me so much?" I ask Vinnie. I just don't get it. I mean why won't guys ask a girl out if they like her!

He looks at me, as I lose myself in his deep brown eyes. "Because I thought that you didn't like me. And a girl like you, I thought, would most probably have a boyfriend." He finally says looking straight into my eyes, in his deep and husky voice.

"What? Are you *crazy*?" I say in utter shock. "You have got to be kidding me." I look at him as he stares at me back with love in his eyes.

"Oh come on! You are trying to tell me that you are unaware of the fact that 9 out of 10 girls working in this office fantasize about making out with you?"

"Really?" He says as he walks towards me.

"…Yes" Oh my God! What did I say? Great! Now I am blushing.

"And do you also happen to have such a fantasy?" he says as he looks at me intensely.

"Aa…yes…"

"Tell me. What is it like?"

Oh come on! He's *got* to be kidding me! But anyway, what's the harm in telling.

"I always imagined it to happen in the store room." I blurt.

"Hmm, the store room, in the dark." He says as he caresses my face.

"Well," I say deliberately making my voice sound a little husky and sensuous, "it's not completely dark, there is always some light, enough light to...

Beep beep, beep beep.

"Oh what is that?" I ask looking around.

He is silent

Beep beep, beep beep.

"What? Is that a truck?" I say irritated, the best moments of my life being swept away by the sounds of a truck. *Is* it a truck? I look around.

The beeping continues. I fumble. No, not a truck; it's my alarm clock! It's a dream! Damn! Its morning! I have to get to work. Sad that I have to get out of the bed. Let me just turn on the computer and put on some music first.

It is such a wonderful morning. I walk to the main door to get the newspaper. I pick it up and without any delay; I fish out the magazine section. Hmm, so what do we have today? HEY!!!! THAT'S RISHIKA'S ARTICLE!!!! They published it. '*The benefits of being a girl in today's world*' WOW!!!! THEY SELECTED HER ARTICLE!!!! I must call her up and tell her. I dash to find my cellphone and call her.

"Hi!" she says.

"*Hello*! So someone's getting published!"

"Yeah, I just saw it too. Thanks." Rishi chuckles. I can almost see her gleaming with joy.

"See, I am telling you. You should take your writing more seriously."

"Hmm, yes. You know, I think I should. And I have been toying with an idea lately. May be I should develop it into a novel. Everyone seems to be writing one these days. Why can't I?"

"Yes! You go girl! Why can't you? And you know I am sure you are going to be better than *all* of them!" Oh, I feel so proud to have such friends. This friend, she is going to become a famous writer. And Amit, he will also soon figure out what kind of celebrity he wants to become. And I, I will be happy being a pop star. We are so going to rock! We are going to make headlines, be all over Page 3. Just like they show in the movies!

"Thank you."

"You are always welcome, love. Now I am going to sit and read your article. Although I have read and edited it like, a thousand times, but I want to read it published in a newspaper."

"Ok" she says.

"Ok then, talk to you later. Bye."

"Bye"

I sit down and read the whole article. I look at my watch and guess what? It seems that I am late again. But how does that matter? It happens every day. It is almost like it has lost all excitement – like an aerated drink minus the fizz. Rushing to office when you are getting late is one thing. These days I don't even feel rushed.

20 minutes later I am still in the shower when I hear the cab honking.

Damn! Never mind. I will go to office on my own today. And you know what, its good in a way; I would be able to pick up my Costa's on the way.

One hour later I enter my office building.

It *is* slightly uncomfortable to reach office when everyone is already in their seats. I sit down and see Vinnie walking towards me. Hmm. Will this be the day? Should I make the first move? I may have had that dream for a reason today. Yes! I am doing it today. Not like *doing it*, doing it and fulfilling my fantasy, but just giving him a hint.

"Hi." I get up as he reaches my workstation.

"Hey! Good morning!"

"Morning," I say with a beaming smile as I tilt my head to a side.

"So, how's the day been so far?"

"The day," I say as I let out a cute little laugh, "has just started. I have just reached office."

"Oh, Cool." He says.

"Hey, listen, I was just thinking… the store room, it's so unorganized. I was thinking we should do something about it. You know, yesterday I went there to get some old files and it was so dark and… you should come with me someday there. I would show you…" now that *was* a hint, was it not? A girl should not be more direct than this.

"Hmm, you are right. Actually I also went there a few days back." What? I missed it?

"But today I am slightly tied up." He says looking at his watch. "But you know, I would report this to the authorities, may be they can send the janitor or someone, and you can direct and instruct him on how to go about it."

What? The janitor? Does this man not get a hint at all? God, I hate these faithful one-woman-type guys!

"Yeah, the janitor… yes, that would be good." uh!

"Ok then, see you around."

"Yeah, see you." I say forcing a smile. Ok. Lesson learnt – next time, I'll be a little more direct.

Amit – Firangs, infidelity and The Bridges of Madison County.

I look at my watch for the millionth time. The play will start at 7:30 PM. It is already 7:20 AND I AM STILL STUCK IN THE TRAFFIC JAM!!!!! Sehar is going to be so mad at me. So what am I doing sitting in this stupid auto? I stick my head out of the auto to see where exactly I am. Hmm, not far. If I run, or walk briskly, I can reach in less than 7 minutes which is cool. I hurriedly hand over the money to the *autowala,* jump out and start running. In less than a minute I realize that I can't run that fast. I have not run for ages. I have so lost the stamina. I stop; panting like a dog, then begin to walk briskly. In five minutes I reach the theatre. It is already dark and I enter the gate and start looking around. Where is she? She can't *not* be here. Oh there she is! I identify her silhouette in the dark. But who is that man she is laughing and talking to? I can't identify him! WHO IS HE? At that point, Sehar spots me. What! Why is he leaving? Where is he going? He is entering the building and … he has vanished.

"Hi! See I made it in time!" I say

She smiles and hugs me.

"Who was that guy with you?" I ask.

"Who? That guy who was just standing here? He was my patient, the one I told you about? I suggested that he should take his wife out more often and he ended up coming to this play too. It turns out that he has the same choice as us." She says as she warmly holds my hand and we walk into the auditorium.

The play is an adaptation of "*Bridges of Madison County*". Nice play but I fail to understand – why everything to do with America always revolves around extra marital affairs? But *Bridges of Madison County* is actually pretty nice. At least the ones having the affair part ways for the good of the family. The play ends and I am almost in tears. I try to hide my face to wipe away my tears and turn to see that Sehar has already stood up.

"Oh come on! Stop crying like a baby. We have got to rush." She says.

"What? No! Why? I mean I was not crying! Like my eyes were a little … damp by the end of it, but I was not like *crying*, crying."

She stares at me with that knowing expression.

"And why do we need to rush?" I ask.

"I just remembered that I left the iron switched on at home."

"WHAT?" I freak out! "You are going to burn the house down one day!"

"No I am not. Now can we hurry?"

In less than five minutes we are inside her house.

"Guess what? It turns out that I was mistaken. I *did* turn it off before I left!" she says. "Stupid me." she smiles.

"Its ok, it happens to all of us." I say putting my hand around her waist.

"Yes." She says as she gently pushes my hand away. "Come on, let's go. It's getting late. I will drop you home."

At times I feel that Sehar is a different woman. Almost like someone I don't know. A few months back she would always insist that I spend the night at her place and now here she was pushing me out of her house!

"Yeah, it is getting late. If you want me to go back home then we must leave."

"Yes, let's leave."

Funny, she does not even get the hint these days.

Rimz – She have to get it all, her love, her life.

Dweepy dumbly...damn! Its 9:30 AM.!!!! I am late again!!!! Do I have 5 minutes to get ready? Or have I missed the cab already? Wait! I will just call someone in the cab and ask. Oh chuck it! I will go myself.

25 minutes later I am out of the bathroom and another 20 minutes later, out of the house dressed in my new Gucci outfit bought in London. I enter the office in my high heels with my Costa a good 20 minutes later. Oh, Vinnie is just seven workstations away from my workstation! I must touch up my makeup *now*. I fish out my compact to see how I look. Gorgeous, as always. With a smile I close the compact and put it in my bag.

"Hey Vinnie!" I call out.

He looks up to see who is calling him. Oh, those innocent eyes! Oh that innocent expression!

"Here, me, here." I wave at him with a generous smile.

"Hi!" he says brightly and comes to my workstation.

"How are you?"

"I am good. How are you?" I say. Oh, I can't take my eyes off him.

"Good." he says nodding.

Silence.

Oh no! I am foolishly staring at him and not uttering a word. Oh no! Not good. I fish around for something to say.

"So have you heard the new Dido song? I know you like her songs." Dido? Is that the best I can do? *Dido*?

"Yes. *'If I don't believe in love'*"

"*'Nothing is good for me'* right?" I sing as I let out a little laugh.

"Yes." He smiles. A smile! Now that is a good sign.

"You know what?" I say after a three seconds pause, "I have the video here on my computer. Do you want to see it?"

"Really? But I believe we are not supposed to keep our personal stuff in the office computers."

"Oh come on! We are into event management. How are we supposed to work if we are clueless about the latest trends, latest fashion?" I run my hand down my dress as I say that "and latest music? And what is so personal about a music video anyway?" I turn around to my computer and reach the folder where I had saved all my favorite videos. "It's so relaxing. When you have like a deadline to meet, take a few minutes off and watch your favorite videos. Well, I watch them all the time here, and getting them into my office computer was my main purpose. I open the folder and…. WHAT THE HELL!!!!!! THE FOLDER IS EMPTY!!! How can this be? Ok, don't freak out now. They must be here somewhere; I must have dragged and dropped them somewhere by mistake. I instantly run a search for my videos on my computer. I turn around to see Vinnie still smiling at me. After a few seconds of silence, the smile now looks a little forced and awkward. He is uncomfortable and he still he won't show his discomfort.

"I must have misplaced the video on my comp. I will just find it in a jiffy!" I say breaking the silence.

"You know," he says a little hesitantly, "I've got to go right now. You find the video. I will see it later, ok?"

"Yeah, sure." I say grinning.

"Ok, catch you later."

"Yeah, sure, catch you." I say almost laughing. Oh how he makes me happy.

I sit down to find Pooja looking at me.

"Hi!" she says.

"Hi"

"I should not be pointing out like this, but this is the third time this week that you are late."

"Oh come on Pooja," I say sounding as casual as ever, "we all know. *It's fine.*"

"And did you have any movies stored in your computer?"

"Oh Pooja, I did not have any *movies* in my comp. I just had one. And a few music videos. But why do you ask?"

"No, it's just that Deepika ma'am caught Ramesh seeing something on your comp this morning. Ma'am was furious at that. She sat herself down and deleted those files."

Oh no! Now I would have to get them again. May be I would put them as hidden files this time. Ramesh wouldn't know how to get to them. Ramesh, by the way is our office peon. Anyway, nosey Pooja has to poke her nose into everything. Hmm, so I should start with the day's work then. Let me check mail first. Hmm what do we have here? Two new mails.

To: Rima Saxena <rima.saxena@iibbcc.in>
From: Human Resources <human.resources@iibbcc.in>
Subject: Tardiness

Dear Rima Saxena,

We have received reports that your work output and efficiency is not up to the mark. We have also received reports that you are generally late for work. This is to remind you that your workday starts at 10 AM. It would be really appreciated if you came to office on time. As part of the Human Resource Department, we desire your complete well being. If there is any problem you face, please feel free to come and discuss it with us.

Best wishes

Human Resource Department IIBBCC

Please note that any tardiness in future may result in suspension or dismissal.

Oh! What crap!

To: Rima Saxena <rima.saxena@iibbcc.in>
From: Human Resources <human.resources@iibbcc.in>
Subject: Music Videos on your work computer

Dear Rima Saxena,

This is to inform you that some non-work related video files were found on your work computer. We would like to remind you that as an office policy, we don't allow our employees to store any personal data in the office computers. We request you to kindly remove all the personal data that you have stored in your work computer and take care that such incidents do not take place in the future.

Best wishes
Human Resource Department IIBBCC

Oh what bull shit!! I really don't understand why they would ask me to 'remove all video files' when they already have removed then. Uh! Dumb!

Amit – The dream job and other confusions of life.

"Amit! I have news for you." It is Rishika, she really sounds excited. She has called me, and from the sounds I can hear in the background, it is pretty evident that she is driving.

"What! Are you marrying the guy you met today?" I say

"No stupid! Just wait till I reach there." Rima and I are at the coffee shop, waiting for Rishi – as part of our evening ritual.

"What surprise is she talking about? She called me ten minutes ago too. I am sure she is going to marry this new guy she met." Rima says.

"I don't know, let's see. Anyway, so how's office?" I ask.

"Hmm, you know, let's not talk about it."

"Ok." I say, taking a sip from my leechi iced tea.

"It's just those… stupid… mails that…that the HR department keeps sending that *boils my blood*. Why can't they just behave like … humans? AND IT'S NOT A CRIME TO KEEP MUSIC VIDEOS IN YOUR COMP IN OFFICE! And even if they have a problem with that then why can't they directly *tell* me? Or … tell me over the phone? Why *mail*? Anyway, forget it. You know, at times I really sit and wonder how we have to just work, work and work against our wishes. You know, it's *so unfair*! Why did God give us all these feelings …and … desires… if we were to lead such mechanical lives in those … tiny … lifeless… cubicles?"

I smile; it was like she had just vocalized what went on in my mind all the time. "So that we can work towards those dreams and desires." I reply.

"No! I don't like it." she says angrily, banging her fists on the arm rests repeatedly like a baby.

"Ok," I say, "tell me. What do you *want* to do in life? Like *want to*, want to do. And not crib about it later. For as I see it, we humans are perpetually cribbing about anything that we would have to do as a 'job'."

"What?" she says, she had hardly paid any attention what I had said in the end.

"What?" I ask

"What *what*?" she says "Don't you know?"

"Know what?"

"What I *want to be* Amit?"

"I know," I say, "but I want to hear it. I want to hear it again."

"I want to be a pop star."

"And?" I ask

"And I want to become the *queen of hearts*." I can already see her dreaming as she smiles and looks at the table with unseeing eyes.

"Anyway, my dreams are clear. You tell me, what would your dream scenario be?"

Hmm, what would my dream scenario be? I think for a minute.

"You know, if you really ask me, I have kind of come to terms with the idea that there is nothing known as a *'dream job'*. Every job would have its own set of problems. But, if I am given a choice, I would… I don't know, do something for the needy may be, for the poor."

"O my God!" she bursts out laughing.

"*What?*" I ask surprised.

"What, *what?* I am not a part of a judges' panel, and you are not here for a beauty pageant."

"No, seriously. That is the only thing I believe, that can bring satisfaction to our mundane lives. I want to help the poor children may be. Do something for the under privileged ones. Maybe start an NGO for them one day."

"Hey! Rishika is here." She almost screams, "Let's ask her."

"What? Ask what?" she says as she settles down.

"Yes, your dream job. What would it be?" Rima asks.

"No job as such. I would only want to be a writer." Rishi says

"Oh come on guys! You got to be joking! He wants to become Mother Teresa, you want to become Arundhati Roy!"

"Hey!" we both say in unison. And then we both fall silent and look at each other.

Then Rishi says, "I don't want to become another *Arundhati Roy*. But I aspire to becoming something like...Cecelia Ahern."

"Yes," I say, "and I never said anything about world peace. I just want to help the poor. Their situation worries me."

"Ah! *Worries* you, you guys. You are so impractical. Seriously, you both live in your dream worlds. *Please*, get *real*!"

Yes, yes. Look who's talking?

"You know what?" Rishi says as she steps completely into her thinking mode, "I feel that the reason why today's generation is experiencing this huge feeling of 'dissatisfying jobs' is because our generation has crossed a barrier. I mean, if we look at our parents' generation, or the generation before that, getting a job and earning a living –was not something very easy. India had recently got independence and was still stabilizing. But the situation is different today. Getting a job is not that big a deal. Neither is making money. So our generation doesn't get satisfied by just making money. They seek satisfaction at different levels now. "

"Yeah, true." I say, still thinking about what Rishi has just said.

"Hey! You know what? You should put this in your book when you write it." Rimz says.

"Yeah, true." I say.

"Hey Rishi, What about the surprise?" Rimz asks.

"Oh yes! The surprise, I completely forgot. I just can't wait to show you what I discovered today." She says as she boots her laptop.

"We have Wi-Fi here right?" She asks

Amit — Web Therapy and its impact on real life.

"Ok. So let's talk about television today. Who have you missed the most on television lately?"

Rima and I look at each other in bewilderment. What is she talking about?

"You know? Our favorite TV character?"

Still no answers.

"Ok. Let's make it simpler. Your favorite TV show?"

"FRIENDS?" we both ask a little confused, looking at each other. Was this the answer she was expecting? what was she getting to?

"Your favorite character?"

"Phoebe!" I scream

"Rachel!" Rima yells.

"Sorry to disappoint you Rima, but Amit, I have the most amazing surprise for you. I discovered, today, that Lisa Kudrow…" she says pausing practically every second as I stare at her with my eyes popping out in excitement. Was Lisa Kudrow coming to India? Was Rishi going to arrange a meeting for us with her? Was I gonna become the luckiest guy in the whole universe?

"…Is doing an Internet show on a website called *WEB THERAPY*.."

"WHAT? When? Where? How?" I scream.

She looks at me with a smile and says, "Behold." And comes and settles next to me on the couch. All three of us line up and watch Lisa say, "*Hi. I am Fiona Walles. And this, is web therapy.*"

Lisa plays a Psychiatrist in the show. It is pretty funny. Instead of talking about the patient she goes on talking about herself. And the patient is someone who she had once tried flirting with. And now he is having some problems with his wife and Lisa seems to be taking the opportunity to just throw herself at him. It is actually hilarious. Rishi and Rima are laughing their guts out.

Rishi turns around, looks at me and as she pops a cherry in her mouth she says, "This is so cool. You know what this reminds me of?"

"What?" I ask.

"You and Sehar when you started going around. She was so much like this when you first met."

Amit – His struggle to get some excitement back in his life. (Don't you think he deserves it?)

This is just not done. I won't let this happen. My life can't be this sad – I am sitting in my bed in the middle of the night and writing in my diary. How frustrating and sad my life has become! No! I won't let the passion between us die. I will do anything to rekindle it. ANYTHING! It used to be so nice initially. You know what? YES! I should do that!!!! Yes!!! Her all time greatest fantasy about someone breaking into her house and… In the dark… mysteriously, and… I am going to break into her house today. In the dark. I will be the mystery man and I will climb up the balcony. In total *Shakespeare in Love* style. YES, it will be *a whole new world* after that.

But it's midnight. How will I reach her house? Oh! I know! The radio cab!!!! I pick up the phone and dial the 'easy to remember' number. The one with many '4's and many '9's. And what do they tell me? The cab will be there to pick me up in twenty minutes!!!! Well, now what will I need? Oh yes! A red rose to hold between my teeth as I climb up the pipe to her balcony. But where will I get it at this time of the night? I KNOW!!! THE NEIGHBOUR'S GARDEN!!! Cool, so everything is set. On the dot in twenty minutes I have the cab honking in front of my house. I run down and sit in it wearing my black tuxedo. In seven minutes I am standing in front of her building. I will have to climb to the second floor. Hmm, its ok, it's manageable. I look at the balcony trying to calibrate the effort I will need to put in. I place the rose between my teeth and aaaaa… what is that? A thorn! Great! Now I have bleeding lip. Uh! But never mind, all in the name of love. I start climbing and remember not to look down.

The pipe!!!! It is ..slippery!!! And I keep getting that horrible thought - the kind of thing they show in all the fantasy movies – the pipe is going to turn into a serpent and then, I will transform the rose into a sword using my magical powers and then … fight. But that is happening only in my head and not in reality. In two minutes I reach the balcony, completely exhausted, thirsty, and sweaty and… oh, believe me, all of you have no idea how tough it is to climb up a pipe to go up a floor. Lifts, staircase and escalators – they are actually worth all the thought, effort and invention. Anyway, so I am finally on the balcony. As I turn around and look inside her room, I see two candles dimly illuminating the place. Hmm, must be a power cut again. And as usual she has left the door unlocked. Stupid girl! She calls herself a psychologist but does not even know one should lock the door in case of a power cut. It is unsafe, and just like extending an invitation to thieves and robbers. Huh! Madam 'I read people's minds'. Such a dum dum she is. But she is my cutie vootie shweety dum dum. Hey! Wait a minute!!! What is that?? I mean who is that? There is someone else in her bed!!!! . And he is!!!! … Oh my God!!! … He is trying to … *rape* her!!! . Oh no!!!! Now I actually need the rose to turn into a sword to fight that villain!!! . And she is screaming too. She is saying *"noo, nooo."* But the guy is going on and on!!! Noooo!!! . Wait my love!! I am here now, *I will save you.* What should I do? What should I do?? I think awhile standing there in the dark. Should I turn on the lights? And see the face of that…villain first? I rush to the switchboard, topple over two tables and turn on the lights.

"AAAA!" Sehar screams.

"AAAA!", the guy screams.

"AAAAAA!", I scream.

Sehar takes a few seconds to understand the scene. And I take a few seconds to perceive that she is nude under the bed sheet. Oh God! Let me see the face of the monster who is… I walk towards the guy with brisk steps pointing the rose at him (I have by now actually come to believe that it is a sword.) He is similarly nude. Shameless… pig!

"*You*!!!!" I roar "You are so dead you…"

"Amit. Wait!" Sehar screams

I freeze and turn around to look at her.

"He is… he is not… uh! He is my patient."

What?

"And we were…"

I am shell-shocked to hear that. Was it a therapy session? Did I misunderstand something? Did I disturb them?

"No, we are, we are…" she looks at him and says, "We are in love." And she let out a long, heavy breath.

Rimz – Love, sex and magic.

Today is the day. It's going to be now or never. I cannot wait anymore. Why is it so tough for him to confess his love for me? I know he loves me. I see it in his eyes like… all the time. It is a beautiful morning. Just look outside, the birds are chirping (although I can't hear them from the other side of the fixed glass window of an air conditioned office building, but I know they are). The flowers are blooming; the sky is the best blue I have seen ever. It's the perfect set up to tell someone that you love him. Oh! Here he comes. Let me just smoothen my hair and just TELL HIM!

"Vinnie, Can I see you for a moment in the store room?" I say. Yes! This is the day! I am going to tell him and then we are going to make out!!! . The final fantasy!!!!! "Yeah, sure." He beams at me. O God! My heart just skips a beat. He is so handsome.

"What happened?" He asks

"Nothing. Just come. I will show you." Show you. *Show you.* Show you what?

"Yes, here. Get inside." God! I sound like a military commander. More like a sex military commander.

"What?" he says with a confused smile as he lets out a little laugh. But he is walking in. That is a good sign. That says he loves me. I shut the door behind us. It is dark.

"What? What's going on?" he asks again.

"Hmm, having fun aren't you?" I say sounding like an irresistible temptress, throwing him against the wall. "This is the day Vinnie. This is the day I tell you that I love you."

"Excuse me?" he says as he tries to slip aside.

"Yes, I love you. And I know you do too. So let us just, get on with it."

"No! I mean yes, I do love you… but… in a very… non-sexual way. I mean… I … like men."

"It's ok," I advance towards him breathing heavily "Even I like men."

"No," he slips a little further away, "I mean I have a different orientation."

Oh no! "You mean… you are … gay?"

"Oh my God! I am … such a fool." I say as I stumble back.

"I am sorry." He says with a smile. Oh! That divine smile!!!

"May be we should do it once. May be that would…" I stammer

He smiles again. Oh that smile, it looks so pure, so … saintly…!

"I am sorry. I should just go." I say I had never been more disappointed. I open the door and see my boss!!! What the hell is she doing here? Can this get any worse? She will surely guess what has just happened… and will fire me. No, wait, she is a very understanding person, may be she would understand.

"Morning, Rima." She says.

"Oh! Hi! I mean morning Deepika! How are you?"

"I am good," she says, and just then Vinnie comes out of the storeroom.

She frowns "What were you two doing inside the store at this time in the morning? And why is your hair all messed up?" she asks

Ah! As if there is some set time to do it in the store! Like not before lunch or something! Uh!

"Actually ma'am... I was showing Vinnie... how tough it is for the housekeepers to... use the store without any lights ... so that we both could... send a request to the HR department to... light up the store." God! Is this the best I could come up with? A request? To the HR department?

"Ok, then. You should... submit that application." She says. "See you around." And she walks away leaving me all red with embarrassment.

Amit – Love dies, love hurts

"My life is over. There was only one thing that was helping me go on with my life and that is also gone now." I say. This is really unfair; Seher should not have done this to me. She should have told me earlier, on her own. I should not have discovered it like this. I feel so... moronic.

"I know! Could life be any worse? This is just not fair!!! There is just one good looking guy in the office that I fall in love with AND HE TURNS OUT TO BE GAY!!!"

Everyone sitting in the cafeteria turns around to look at Rima.

"Uh! It is so irritating. What the hell is their problem! Morons! These morons will never understand how I feel. How many of them have ever fallen in love with a person of a different sexual orientation?" She groans.

"It's ok Rima. Calm down. It's not like someone you were committed to betrayed you. Look at Amit. He is calm. He is taking the whole betrayal so well." Rishika says.

"Calm? Calm? Is that how I look right now?" I question.

May be its good in a way that my feelings are not synchronized with my expressions. For who would like to look stupid? Yes that is how I am feeling right now – stupid. One has to be a fool not to understand all the signs and clues. It is all so obvious. And I trusted Sehar. Fool!! Fool!!

"Oh come on Amit! Now don't get upset about it now." Rishi says as she looks at my changing expressions. "And it's only good that you got rid of that Zehar called Sehar." She breaks into peals of laughter.

I give her an angry look and she stops laughing.

"Ok ok. I won't make fun of her, your *ex-love*. But come on guys! Even I am in a very tight situation. That does not mean we should sit here with faces so long that they touch the floor."

It is not funny. But I know how it feels when no one laughs at your joke – it happens with me all the time. So I let out a little laugh.

"*Vasay* what is the situation like? I mean, are you guys telling your parents?"

"Hmm, well I guess we have to. We can't delay it any further. Iman is leaving for Lucknow the day after tomorrow to talk to his parents. And I am leaving tomorrow."

"Hmm. So you have informed the office?"

"No. I am just going to call in sick." She says

"You know what? I am also going to do that. I mean not going home and telling my parents that I threw myself at someone and he turned out to be gay, but just call in sick and go home for a few days."

"Hmm, so that means that I would be all alone here in Gurgaon for… how long?"

"4 days." Rishi says.

"Yes, 4 days should be good". Rima says as she nods and makes a decision.

Amit – More of his dreadful meetings at office.

"Amit the meeting starts at 11. You know that, right?" Shobha with her usual I-am-the-boss-remember-that? expression.

"Yes ma… Shob." I say

'Ha ha ha" she laughs, "now I am *your* Shob is it?"

"No… Shob, I didn't mean that…"

"Its ok just put the presentation together. It's very important that we present the design in the best way possible today."

"Yes Shob."

"Good. See you at 11 in the conference room then." And she exits with her heels clicking on the floor.

I really don't know where the world is heading. Humans are destroying the world like none else. Haven't they seen the changes in the global climatic patterns? I mean what more do they want? Isn't global warming scary enough? But *no*! Who cares? We would make a *home away from home*, destroying every little bit of natural environment that we are left with. And then crib about how warm the summers are becoming each passing year! Anyway. How does it matter? I can't stop them single-handedly if the whole bloody, international firm is hell-bent on making another Shanghai along the Aravalli foothills! I am just a little pawn on the board. I should perhaps go with the flow! I should just … stick my nose to the computer screen and prepare the presentation!

I enter the conference room dot at 11 AM. Every time I set up the projector and the laptop my anxieties and … dipping levels of confidence make me doubtful about the process – I always manage to plug in the cables right but is it F5, or F4 or some other F that I need to press to get the images projected from the laptop on to the screen. And which button do I press on the projector? And for how long should I keep my finger on the power button?

But, like every time though, it magically happens bang on schedule before everyone comes into the conference room.

Once the people settle down, I notice a weird vibe all around. Everyone seems to be more serious today. There are no jokes being cracked and no one is laughing before the boss enters the conference room. He also has a kind of grave expression on his face. Everyone stands up as he walks into the room. He nods and everyone sits following his cue. No one says a word and stares curiously at the boss – as if he is going to drop a bomb or something.

He takes a deep breath and starts speaking,

"As we all know, the world has been hit by the global meltdown."

What? The Polar Ice Caps have started melting? Oh no. The sea levels are now going to rise and we are all going to drown and … Oh no!

"And our company has also been affected." He continues.

OH NO!! The world is ending!! Oh no!!!

"The recession is strong."

Recession? What the hell is that? Now I must figure that out. I must keep myself up-to-date about all the environmental issues. I immediately scribble in my notepad

— *must google recession.*

Shob shoots a look at it and whispers in my ear, "Don't you know that the world economy has been hit? The recession? It's all over the newspapers. Don't you read the newspaper?"

No I don't! I don't know a thing about it. And why should I read the newspapers anyway? There is nothing good in them. So and so died, so and so attacked, so and so killed herself, such and such bomb blast...It would only take a person from a state of depression (which most of us are in, these days) to a higher one and then just push us over the edge.

"Shob, what are you whispering in your assistant's ear? I have bad news for you." Boss says.

SHOBHA'S ASSISTANT!!!! I AM NOT SHOBHA'S ASSISTANT!!! Shobha sits up straight in her chair. She does not utter a word. She looks back at him with the most nervous expression ever.

"Our client for the development project, that you were handling, has terminated the project."

"Oh no!" she lets out a sigh of distress.

"And that is not all. A lot of our clients are doing that." He scans the room and continues. "And we have been forced to downsize our firm."

What? What the hell is going on? The project has been terminated. Some global recession has … erupted. And we are downsizing? HAS THIS MEETING BEEN CALLED ONLY TO TELL US THAT WE ARE BEING FIRED??!!!! OH MY GOD!!! I AM SOO FIRED!! BOSS IS GOING TO TELL SHOBHA, I DON'T THINK WE CAN AFFORD YOU AND YOUR ASSISTANT ANYMORE!!! OH NO! OH NO!!!!

"But fortunately, he continues, "no one present in this room would be asked to leave."

'Except you Amit. Not only because we are downsizing, but also because you have been a nuisance here always!!!' Oh no! He is going to say that. OH NO!! I stare at him with my eyes bulging like balloons. I catch his eye.

"Yes," he says. Oh no! OH NO!! "Not even you."

"What? Why? I mean … ok." I mumble. Good God! Did I just say that??!! DID I JUST SAY THAT???!!!!! Did I just ask him why am I not being fired?

"Yes, because it's rare to come across passionate people. And you would be lesser trouble, working here for us; then working with some *NGO*, trying to shut us down."

What? What did that mean? Should I be thankful to him for not kicking me out? Or should I take it offensively? I really didn't know what to say.

"Thank you sir." I say with a smile.

"It's ok." He turns away. "The HR department will mail all the people whose services will not be required henceforth. I wanted all of you guys to be kept in the loop. The meeting is over." He gets up and leaves.

What? This is it? No presentation? No projector? Uh! What a waste!

Chatting, just like the way you guys do it.

Rishi is online.

Amit : *What the hell is recession!*

Rishi : *Yes Amit, I reached home fine. And I had a pleasant journey as well. Thank you for asking.*

Amit : *Ok, that is good. By the way, did you tell your parents?*

Rishi : *Not yet. I didn't want to just land and bombard them with hard and difficult to digest information. I am going to tell them tomorrow.*

Amit : *Ok, great. Did you know about this recession?*

Rishi : *Yes Amit I did. Just like every other sane, normal and literate person on this planet.*

Amit : *Really? Then how could I have missed that out? Anyway. You know, everyone is saying that there is no money anywhere. But what I don't understand is where did all the money go? I mean everyone had the money right? It was being transferred from one hand to the other. It was physically present – the currency notes! Where did it all suddenly vanish???*

Rishi : *Hmm, Ok, contrary to your beliefs and presumptions, the reality is different. Not all the money is present in the form of the currency notes. A huge chunk of it lies in the stocks. The actual state and story only economists can tell you. But how I would explain it is that some big people made some very wrong decisions and suffered the biggest losses. And the world economy came crumbling down.*

Amit : *hmm, does not make much sense to me. I still don't understand how money can disappear.*

Rishi : *It did not disappear, it…*

Amit : *Anyway, I also googled global recession today. They have quite fancy alternative names for it as well – global melt down and all which sounds like some repercussion of Global Warming. And that does make more sense to me coz I can see that the world is heading towards a terrible end coz we destroyed the environment so much, that the economy crumbled first, and then the rest of the world. 2012 – its more then just a movie.*

Rishi : *yes, yes. You and your stupid phattas.*

Amit : *no, I also came across this news article*

Rishi : *Really? Is this Amit I am talking to? The one who I went to college with?*

Amit : *Yes, and it talked about how Hollywood reacts in such scenarios. During the last deep recession that happened in the*

Rishi : *yes, now you are talking. This makes more sense – movies.*

Amit : *yes, and the last deep recession that happened in the 50's led Hollywood to make cheerful, happy and feel-good musicals which would uplift peoples' spirits. And the article said that Hollywood is exhibiting such a trend again by making movies* like Mamma Mia and High School Musical and stuff. Actually… it was a film review of Mamma Mia.

Rishi : *hmm, no wonder you read it.*

Amit : *yes, and I was happy to know that there was one good thing this recession brought with itself – good cheerful, uplifting musicals.*

Rishi : *hmm, good.*

Amit : *by the way, Meryl Streep rocks!*

Rishi : *Yes, go marry her.*

Amit : *hmm, I am seriously going to give it a thought*

Rishi : *yes, you do that. I gtg now, mom calling for dinner.*

Amit : *ok, cool. Happy eating.*

Rishi : *Yes, happy eating to you too.*

Amit : *thnx, I will see u online tomorrow.*

Rishi : *ok*

Amit : *Bye, I also need to eat now.*

Rishi : *bye*

Amit ; *Bye.*

Rimz – There is a solution for every problem (oh yes, there so is!)

I am broken hearted again. There is only one person in this whole world that can help me – my idol – the goddess - Madonna. I am going to take out the CD and randomly play a song. And try to meditate. Oh! *Borderline*. Ok, now let me meditate. The lyrics so aptly talk about my condition right now.

Stop playing with my heart
Finish what you start
When you make my love come down
If you want me let me know
Baby let it show
Honey don't you fool around

Chorus

Borderline feels like I'm going to lose my mind
You just keep on pushing my love
Over the borderline

But this is not helping. There has to be a hint... a clue in this song. Hmm, borderline, borderline... what does it mean? YES! I GET IT.! HE IS A BORDERLINE CASE!!! HE IS NOT GAY! I can turn him around. Yes! I can use the power of media for that. I will make him watch some movies. Some nice, mushy, romantic comedies. That will influence him. After all he belongs to the same generation as I, one that is extremely influenced by the media. Our lives are *governed* by the media. We want to do all that they do in the movies *exactly the same way*. Oh this is so workable. I can already see the results. I can visualize it. Just the way '*Secret*' (the book that changed the lives of millions the world over. And most of all those of the authors) did. I must visualize that he is not gay. No! No mention of gay. I need to get it out of my mind. Or else I would be 'vibe-ing' it back. I must visualize him straight. I must make a visualizing board so that five years from now I can stumble upon a box unexpectedly and narrate this wonderful story to a friend, *or maybe* my kid, with tears of joy in my eyes. Yes! YES! Ok, now that all of this is sorted out, I must treat myself to a pizza and a good T.V show. I turn on the T.V and start surfing the channels. Hey! What is that on Pony Television!!! It's a new talent hunt competition. For singers and dancers. It's called *Come On India Sing And Dance!* Oh my God! I am going to get myself enrolled. WOW! Watch out showbiz! Here I come! Great. I feel so completely renewed. Not only have I found a way to free my love from the evil clutches of a different sexuality, but have also have taken a step closer to my dreams. YEAH!

Amit – How he hates it when he receives his phone bills.

Enter my room and a strong feeling hits me – when the hell am I ever going to clean the room? Just look at the mess here. As if things are not bad enough in life. And what is this weird smell? Good God! Is night before last's *Paneer Butter Masala* still in this room? God! I must find that out. I close the door and notice a red and white envelope on the floor. The postman has slid my 'X phone' bill under the door. I pick it up and tear open the envelope.

Previous Balance	Payments	Adjustments	This month Charges	Amount Payable by IMMEDIATE	Amount Payable after Due Date
3,900.00	- 1500	- 500	+ 2,584.72	4,484.72	4,559.72

Good God! A phone bill of *four thousand five hundred and fifty nine rupees and seventy two paise*! Who the hell have I been talking to? I have spent more than four thousand bucks talking to a girl who has cheated on me and been unfaithful. Could I have been any more stupid? Anyway, there is no way I can pay this bill this month. The X phone company will have to wait. I have already spent most of my salary. If I keep going at this rate, I will never be able to save enough money to buy an I-pod. And God! Just look at the floor! There is no space to even step in anywhere! Its eight now. Rishi must be online. She was supposed to talk to her parents today. Must go online and figure out how things went. I clear off all the empty packets of chips and the chocolate wrappers from my keyboard and turn on my computer.

Well, guess what? She is online!

Amit : *Hi*

Rishi : *Haaai.*

Amit : *O God! Is everything OK?*

Rishi : *Yeah.*

Amit : *hmm. Then why do u sound like a cow?*

Rishi : *hain? What do u mean?*

Amit : *nothing. So how did it go? Did u tell ur parents?*

Rishi : *Yeah*

Amit : *and?????*

Rishi : *It was cool. They agreed and all.*

Amit : *Rishi, I want u to get this loud and clear. TELL ME EVERYTHING IN DETAIL WITHOUT MISSING ANYTHING OUT!*

Rishi : *hmm. Ok. U asked for it. I was playing with Buzoo when Dad came and sat on the middle chair in the lobby. Leaving one chair vacant on each side. U know the chair – the cane furniture thing we have in the lobby?*

Amit : *yes*

Rishi : *yeah, so Dad came and sat on that and picked up the newspaper and started reading it. By then Buzoo had gotten bored of chewing my foot and had headed for my hands. Just then Mom came with bowl full of potatoes, sat down on the chair that was on Dad's right hand side, and stared peeling the potatoes. I identified the opportunity and distracted Buzoo by giving him a ball and got my hands free. I got up and went and sat on the chair that was lying vacant on the left hand side to Dad. Now all the three chairs were occupied.*

Amit : *hmm. Ok. Then?*

Rishi : *then, I cleared my throat.*

Amit : *good. then?*

Rishi : *and said 'Dad, Mom, I want to tell you something.'*

Amit : *then?*

Rishi : *then there was silence. No one said anything. Mom continued peeling the potatoes, and Dad flipped to the next page of the newspaper. And after some 7 seconds, said 'so, you have finally realized that you have found someone.'*

Amit : *O GOD! HE GUESSED IT! OH GOD! THEN WHAT DID U SAY?*

Rishi : *I didn't say anything. I was too shocked to say anything. So there was more silence, this time a longer one, of about some 15 seconds or something. The only sound heard was of the potatoes being peeled, echoing in the room. I must have gulped some 80 times during that silence.*

Amit : *Good God! Your throat must have dried. Then?*

Rishi : *yes, my throat did feel strained, like something was pulling it back in or something.*

Amit : *God!!! Then?*

Rishi : *then he spoke up again 'is it Amit or is it Iman?'*

Amit : *WHAT? HE SUSPECTED U AND I WERE GOING AROUND? THEN WHAT DID U SAY?*

Rishi : *Amit is that a rhetorical question?*

Amit : *...aaaaaa no.*

Rishi : *he said we must get married within six months.*

Amit : *O!*

Rishi : *What O! Do u realize what month is it?*

Amit : *...January?*

Rishi : *yes, and do u understand what it means?*

Amit : *...? ...that it's winter?*

Rishi : *O God! U are such a duffer! That means that we have to get married latest by June. And that means we should have a decent house and a decent set up by that time as all the relatives would want to see how I would be living after I get married.*

Amit : *Oh!*

Rishi : *yes, and that means that I have to make a lot of money in this time.*

Amit : *OH NO!*

Rishi : *yes, AND ITS NOT ENOUGH TIME TO MAKE THE KIND OF MONEY I WILL NEED.*

Amit : *OH NO!*

Rimz – Its time to get back to normal life. So lets go shopping!!!!

"I am completely renewed." I say all breezy and cheerful, with a new zest for life embedded in me. "Not only have I found out a way to win back my love from the evil clutches of the opposite sexuality, but I have taken a step closer to my dreams!"

"That is nice to know." Rishika smiles, "and how are we going to do that?"

"See, I am going to start talking to Vinnie more, become his best buddy. Make him invite me for dinner every weekend, and watch nice mushy, feel-good rom coms with him. And them – BOOM! Make him realize that he has fallen in love with me and then we will live happily ever after. Everything is going to be just like they show in the movies!"

"Great!" Rishika grins

"I also have a list of movies that we would be watching together. You want to see?" I say as I take out my pink notebook and hand it to Rishika.

"Nice." She says as she glances through the list. "So, this is how your dream of being with Vinnie will become true, right?"

"Da*han*?" Oh God! Why the hell is everyone around me so dumb? "See, that is how I am going to be with the one I love. But that is not my dream. My dream is different. Now come on Rishika! Don't you ever listen to me? How many times have I told you that my dream is to become a *pop star*?"

Oh by the way, I haven't told you where I am. I am back in Gurgaon. And so is Rishi. But we both bunked work this morning and instead spent time shopping in the malls!!!! . Isn't that exciting? We are at Shopper's Stop and so far I have bought 3 perfumes and 4 different nail paints, and Rishi has bought one handbag and a pair of shoes. We girls rock don't we? Right now we are on the escalator on our way to the second floor – to the clothes section!!!!!! . Life rocks, I tell you!!! "Yeah, so you signed a contract with a music company is it?"

"No, stupid. Although I can do that any day, as Mr Malik, the head of the marketing department of W music, is like Dad's best friend. And he knows everyone there and can get me signed up in no time. But I want to make it on my own. So, yesterday, I filled up the form, …for…"

Rishi looks back at me "For?"

"*Come on India Sing and Dance*!!! The greatest talent hunt and reality show ever on Indian Television."

"Oh you must be kidding me"

"No! It's true! And the auditions start next week."

"Great! So what song are you preparing?"

"Are you kidding me? Don't you know? Can there be any song, other than *Like a Virgin*? Madonna is a goddess. As long as I have her blessings, there is nothing in this world that can stop me from becoming a Pop Star!"

"Oh God. I am so happy for you." she says as she hugs me. Suddenly we hear some whistling sounds and the escalators halt.

I look around slightly shocked and annoyed and see a security guard waving at us.

"What?" I give him a questioning look.

He continues to whistle waving his hands frantically in air. Seriously, now I just can't understand what is wrong with this fellow.

"I think Rima he is trying to tell us that, we are not supposed to hug on the escalator. That is why…"

"Oh! Then he should say so! Stupid fellow!"

We are in the clothes section and going through the collection of tops they have when it strikes me that I have been very stupid and self involved and have not even asked how things were with Rishi at home.

"Hmm, things are fine" she tells me, "Mom or Dad didn't over react or anything. It's just that we have to get married by June this year."

"WHAT?" I ask, shocked. "This is not our age to get married. We are not old. We are children. We… are… children. Not… ready-to-get-married men and women."

"Yes." She says continuing to browse the tops hanging on the transparent hangers.

"NO! NO, NO, NO, NO, NO, NO. NO, Rishi. This is not right. You must do something about it. Wait, I will find a way. We have to stop this from happening."

"It's ok Rimz. One day or the other I will have to get married. And if I know who I am going to marry, then why delay it?"

"No Rishi! No! It's not your time yet!!!!" God I sound as if she is going to die or something!!! "You have done … nothing in your life!!! You have not even written a book yet!!! . You know everyone writes a book before they get married these days! Have you forgotten that? That is what is in fashion the most."

She stops going through the tops and looks at me, "you know what? You have been pushing me so much to write a book, I think… it's high time that I start that now. As it is my life can't get any more dramatic then it is right now. I think I should just write a novel that explores the dilemmas a modern woman goes through in a metropolitan set up these days. But I am not really sure."

"YES!" I shout out in joy! "See. Now you are talking!!!! . You should do that!!!!!" I say as I imagine Rishi as an award winning authoress, nothing less than the winner of the Booker Prize. As she collects her award, and delivers her Thank You speech, I imagine her mentioning my name and giving me special credit because I was the one who had urged her to follow her heart.

"What time is it?" she suddenly asks, interrupting my thoughts

"7:30" I say, still smiling at my thoughts.

"Come, let's go, Amit must have reached the coffee shop."

Amit – He has issues with marriage too.

"You know what! We all should get married!!! I don't want to get married alone. You guys have five months to find the people who you are going to marry."

"Hmm, not me" I say, taking a deep breath, "I am through with my share of women."

"OK, so you can find a guy for yourself. Rimz can help you with that." and they both burst out laughing.

"Very funny" I say. It is *not* funny. "And anyway, I don't want to have a regular *boring* wedding. If I do get married, whenever that is, I will elope and get married."

"What! Are you out of your mind?" Rimz says, "You won't get to wear all those fancy clothes! And there would be no pictures clicked. No 'turn slightly to your left, …yes! Now smile' sessions. It would be awful."

"Hmm, but it would be more fun to elope with my beloved, go to some hill station, may be … Mussoori! And get married in a small temple on a hill, with you guys as witnesses. It would be drizzling lightly outside. Wouldn't that be great? Just the way they show in the movies? I would drive a bike up the hill with her sitting behind me."

Rishi bursts out laughing, "Yes, you, riding a bike! Sure!"

"Why? Why can't that be? I will learn to ride. And that will be all the preparation I need to do for my wedding."

Then there is silence. I don't know about the rest – what they are thinking. But what I am thinking is – are we really prepared to get married? Are we really ready? And thinking about myself, will I ever be ready? Right now more than anything else, I need to figure out what I am doing with my life? And where am I headed? And what do I actually want to do with my life? And if I am not clear about these two things, how can I take up the responsibilities that come with marriage? God! Doing that would be like killing all my dreams and aspirations! And at so many levels! I mean… I can do anything I want now. Go travelling anywhere alone. Switch a job anytime I want. I can freely think of alternative careers. And …so many other things! But will I be able to do all that after marriage? GOD! The mere thought of it sends shivers down my spine.

Amit — He does not know, but there are people who can read other people's minds.

Boss has gone mad! Never before have we had so many meeting so frequently. God knows what we are going to discuss today. Anyway, why do I care? I just need to connect this projector to this stupid laptop and then just sit there like a dud till the meeting gets over. There is hardly anything that I will be doing here (apart from shading the squares in my note pad). Hmm, and this projector, hmm, maybe I should stay back in office someday and pretend to be working and sneak into the meeting room and watch a movie here. But which movie? Hmm. Maybe *Godzilla*. It will be fun watching that monster on a rampage as Reporters run after it with their cameras and mics. Hmm, or may be *E.T* –little Drew Barrymore, bike ride with the alien was real cool. Just remembering the scene gives me goose bumps. *Or*, maybe I should get a little serious in life and try watching *Gone with the Wind*. The full movie this time. No! Bad idea again, like every time, I will fall asleep and then, wake up only in the morning to find everyone standing and staring at me, including Boss, with a letter in his hand that will most politely state that I AM FIRED! No, no, no! Very bad idea! But which movie can I watch? Ok, I can do one thing. Put this on my to-do list.

—   *Figure out which movie to see when I sneak into the office meeting room and pretend to be working late.*

"Amit, are we done with the set up?"

Oh no! It's Shobha!!!! .

"Yes Ma'am ...Shob. Almost done..."

I say as I slam shut my organiser.

Damn!

"Good. Boss is on his way."

I set up the stuff. And with a very serious expression I take my seat. No, I don't have anything to worry about. No one knows what I am thinking. I know some people say that they can read people's minds, but they just say it, just like that. There is no person in this whole world who can actually read someone else's mind. Not even Shobha. I pull back my favorite chair and sit down; it will be most difficult for Boss to spot me if I sit here. I can doze off even as he continues yapping.

"Hi Amit. How are you?" It's Harry, one of my colleagues.

"I am good, how are you?" I reply with a smile that we beam every time we open our mouths to talk to someone. Its a corporate thing.

"Good. So, seen any movie lately?"

No, no. No, no. I am just being paranoid. How can he know? *He does not know what I was thinking.*

'No, nope. None lately. Not even planning on watching one anytime soon."

I can see a frown on his face. Yes, I can surely make him believe that I am not up to something.

Suddenly everyone gets up. Boss is inside the room now. He walks with brisk steps to his seat, nods and sits. Everyone sits in an almost synchronized motion.

"As we all know, recession has hit the economy." He starts. Uh! How many times is he going to tell us that? Stop boring us already.

"The other board members and I have been thinking about solutions and ways to make our firm survive. Yes, the rumors are true. We are going to close some departments."

Oh! There have been rumors? That is new to me. But not everyone around me seems to be as uninformed.

I hear some people gasping in fright.

"Yes, it's true." He confirms. "And in order to revive our other departments, we are starting a big venture".

I hear more gasps. God! How dramatic can people get?

"We will be buying a piece of land next to the Multanpur Lake. There is a huge piece of land lying vacant there. We will build a luxury resort there. That will be our first resort in a chain of such resorts."

What? Has he gone crazy? That area is home to a species of endangered migratory birds that come every year from places like Russia and God alone knows where else!!! . These people just can't destroy their habitat like that!!!!

Suddenly everyone starts to applaud.

"Excellent idea, sir." Someone says.

"Wonderful sir." Someone else says.

I need to do something. I have to save the birds. I must save the environment!!!! ….the dying world!!!!

"But sir that area is … a natural reserve." I say. It is almost like an involuntary action, something I utter without any notion of what I am saying.

Boss clears his throat and says, "No, it's not. We have checked with the authorities. It's not a natural reserve."

"*Technically* it is not, Boss. But the investigations are on. The Indian Wildlife Association will get the bill passed soon and that area will become a reserve."

"No, that won't happen." He says smiling deviously. "We are faster than them"

"But Boss that area is of great ecological importance –"

"We know Amit," he interrupts me, "and that is why we have decided to make you the project leader for this project."

I hear more dramatic gasps. This time I think I can hear Shobha gasping as well. There is pin drop silence for a few seconds.

"So that we have the best ecological and environment friendly design." He continues as he smiles and looks around.

"Boss we humans are the most powerful and the most intelligent beings on this planet. And therefore we have the greatest responsibility also – of protecting and preserving the world we live in. This piece of land asks us not to touch it. If at all we should do something about this land, we should help the Wildlife Association make it a certified wildlife reserve."

Silence.

"Amit you are being emotional. You must learn that profession and emotions don't go together."

"I am only being ethical Boss."

Silence.

I look around and see everyone staring at me.

"As an employee of this firm I forward a motion to pass this project. People who agree shall raise their hands."

I look around for some thirty seconds in complete horror and shock. Not a single hand is raised.

Rishika – This can't be happening.

The alarm clock starts beeping. 7 AM already! I fiddle with the side table to grab the alarm clock and turn the alarm off. I let out a little groan, "Why the hell do I need to work?" I say out loud and drag myself out of the bed. I remind myself, "I *need* the money."

In thirty minutes I am standing in front of my office building. I force myself to smile cheerfully as I walk through the corridors to my cabin. I have come early to the office today, so that I can complete all pending work. By 9:30 AM, when everyone starts coming and settling at their desks, I am well informed about everything.

Suddenly my phone rings.

"Hello." I say.

"Rishika can I see you in my office?" it's Mr Arun Kumar. The boss.

"Sure, I will be right there." I say brightly.

I push the white door of Arun's spotless white office and enter his cabin.

"Hi Rishika. How are you?" he asks.

"I am good Arun. How are you?"

"I am good." He says clearing his throat. There is an awkward silence in the room.

"Rishika, as you know, there is a global meltdown." Arun continues.

"Yes. Arun." I say slowly, I can sense something is wrong.

"…And our firm has also been affected."

I nod and sit stiffly in my chair. All the muscles in my body have never felt more strained.

"And we were forced to cut down on a few posts in our firm."

"Ok."

Silence.

"I am sorry Rishika. I really tried my best to reason with the authorities. But you know how the corporate world is."

"I understand Sir." I nod with a blank expression on my face. This news is a bolt from the blue. ... this can't be happening! No! I have a fantastic record in this firm and have always managed to pull off things when everyone has given up. There is no way they could fire me!

"The company will give you two months' salary. But they don't expect you to come to office." Arun pauses for a while and then struggles with a smile to comfort me, "I am really sorry Rishika. I will do everything I can to help you. And if there is any job opportunity that I get to hear of, I assure you, I will let you know. And I'll give a strong recommendation"

There is another awkward pause and then Arun continues,

"But my superiors have asked me to reassure you that the firm acknowledges your dedication and efforts, and if in future your present post opens again, you will be our first preference."

"Thanks Arun." I force myself to smile. Whatever it is, I must accept this gracefully.

Rimy – Her fresh and renewed life.

Oh no, the alarm again! I will have to get up and get ready. Wait. Let me put on *Vogue* to pump up energy. Just look at it, the song has started and I feel so sprightly! Today I am going to get ready the way Elizabeth Shue gets ready in the opening credits of *Adventures in Babysitting* – I am going to dance my way into my clothes. Oh yes! I start to dance and choose my best looking clothes. You know, what good are we doing to ourselves if we don't make ourselves feel good by wearing our favorite clothes? Like this pink top and this white skirt?

I am so back on track. I haven't even missed my cab today. And after ages I am on time for work. Anyway, let's just see what has happened while I was gone. Let's switch on the computer. Hmm, I don't know why the hell we have such ancient computers in the office. It takes like a decade to start.

Oh! Look at all these e-mails I have received. Hmm, let's check them one by one. Ok, the first one is from the Human Resource Department. Uff! Don't they have anything better to do in life than to keep sending me mails? They can irritate anyone to death. Anyway, let's see what it says.

To: Rima Saxena <rima.saxena@iibbcc.in>
From: Human Resources <human.resources@iibbcc.in>
Subject: Tardiness
Dear Rima Saxena,

According to our observations, you have not been able to make it to your workstation by 11AM today. We would like to remind you that this is being recorded in your yearly performance report which forms the basis of your appraisal and promotion.

Best wishes
Human Resource Department IIBBCC

Please note that any tardiness in future may result in suspension or dismissal.

Uh! What nonsense! How can they expect everyone to be in office by 11!

To: Rima Saxena <rima.saxena@iibbcc.in>
From: Human Resources <human.resources@iibbcc.in>
Subject: Absence

Dear Rima Saxena,
It has been observed that you have been absent today till the lunch time. Since we have not got any kind of message or notification about your absence, we are marking you absent for the full day.

Best wishes
Human Resource Department IIBBCC
Please note that any tardiness in future may result in suspension or dismissal.
Bull shit! As if I care!

Oh! The next mail is again from HR! What a surprise!
To: Rima Saxena <rima.saxena@iibbcc.in>
From: Human Resources <human.resources@iibbcc.in>
Subject: Absence

Dear Rima Saxena,

It has been noted that you have been absent for the second consecutive day without any notice or notification. We would like to bring it to your notice that if such behavior prevails, it might have some serious consequences.

Best wishes
Human Resource Department IIBBCC
Uh!!! Utter bullshit!

To: Rima Saxena <rima.saxena@iibbcc.in>
From: Human Resources <human.resources@iibbcc.in>
Subject: Absence

Dear Rima Saxena,

It is to bring to your notice that this is the third consecutive day of your absence without any message or notification. We here at the Human Resource Department are worried and wonder if everything is all right with you. We have been trying to call you on your phone as well but we get the switched off recorded message. Please contact us as soon as possible.

Best wishes
Human Resource Department IIBBCC

Flying bull shit!

To: Rima Saxena <rima.saxena@iibbcc.in>

From: Human Resources <human.resources@iibbcc.in>
Subject: Team decision.

Dear Rima Saxena,

We would like to inform you that there was a special meeting
called yesterday to discuss your case. Since we have not
received any reply from you after the repeated queries we sent, it
was decided that the Human Resource Department should
evaluate your performance for the past one year. After the
evaluation report was submitted, a decision was taken that the
firm would not need your services anymore. All your dues have
been cleared and managed in your salary account.

It was a pleasure to have you working with us here at IIBBCC.
We wish you all the best for your future.

Best wishes
Human Resource Department IIBBCC

Flying ... inter galactic bullshit!!!

Uh! And who needs their job anyway? I came here today primarily
to tell them that I am resigning, as I need to leave for Kolkata in two
days for my auditions for *Come on India Sing And Dance*! Anyway.
So, what all can I take with me? Let's see, this coffee mug saying 'I
am a diva', these plastic Disney stickers –

"Rima? You are here? Thank God! And are you all right?"

Ah! It is Pooja. The ever-hyper-for-no-reason Pooja.

"Hi." I say

"You have no idea how worried I was about you. Where were you?

And why was your phone switched off? I must have called you a thousand times!"

"Yes, I had switched my phone off. What else are you supposed to do when you are heartbroken?" I say

"What? Heartbroken? What happened?" she asks surprised.

Oh my God! I am such a fool! What did I just blurt out?

"Yes, heartbroken." Think Rimz think! "Because… my cat ate … my flower … which … my boyfriend gave me for our first anniversary." What?! Is that the best I can come out with?

"Oh!" Pooja seems really stuck for words and unable to react "I am really sorry to hear what they did to you Rima. It is so unfair!" she finally manages to say.

"I know. They don't have any considerations for human emotions. I was in depression, that is why I wasn't coming to office. But whatever, it doesn't really matter. I came to submit my resignation today, anyway."

"Really? Is everything ok?"

"O yes. It's just that I am going to get my first break. Anyway, see you around sometime." I say striding ahead.

"Rimz!" someone calls me from behind. Wait a minute, I know that voice. It's Vinnie. Oh God! No, no! I am not prepared! I am not prepared with the movie list and I can't bear to see his face again. Its heartache - pure and sharp.

"Hi!" I say forcing a dazzling smile as I twirl around, swinging my hair.

"Hi! I am so sorry…" he says. He has never looked more nervous. Is it a good sign? Is he going to propose to me? Has he realized after that day's incident that he is attracted to me, is actually straight and in love with me and just a little tangled up in the mind?

"… To hear what they did to you!" he continues.

Uh! Him too, It's no love; it's only a stupid concern that he has for me.

"And I have also been transferred to Bangalore."

"Really? Good for you!" Heartache! Sharp … piercing heartache!! But I say that as cheerfully as I possibly can. And I actually deliver the expression very convincingly. I am telling you, I do have great acting skills and I can see a bright future for myself in front of the cameras. But am I never to see him again?

"If there is any kind of help that you need, just let me know. I will only be a phone call away."

"Yeah... Sure." I nod.

"And I know that this thing is not going to get you down. You are a strong woman. And you are going to go a long way."

Oh! At least he acknowledges that I am a woman. Uh! Who am I kidding? That is the whole problem in the first place…that he sees me as a woman. That is the reason why he won't go around with me.

Part Two

Amit – how can things keep on falling apart like that?

"What? I can't believe that no one supported you. Anyway then, what happened?" Rimz sounds more concerned than I am about the whole situation.

"Then what? I resigned."

"WHAT?" Rimz and Rishi scream almost in sync.

"Yes." I say coolly taking a sip from my coffee.

"Are you right in the head Amit? Do you know its recession time out there? People are getting laid left, right and center!" Rishi says pointing out of the huge glass window.

I look taken aback.

"She means people are being laid off." Rishi cuts in.

"Oh"

"Yes, that's what I meant. But…" Rimz looks utterly confused as she goes on, "…people are being fired; they are not re*signing*."

"You mean he is lying?" Rishi says as she lets out a little laugh.

"Hey! I am not lying. I did not get fired. I resigned. Everyone saw me doing that! It's just that... it was so... frustrating to see all those dumb cowards sitting there, people who could not even look me in the eye because they were too scared to stand up for what they knew was right." I say taking a bite of the garlic bread. "And my God! What is with this garlic bread? Is it made of rubber or dough? Who can tell? You know what is worse than recession? This garlic bread!" I say. God! Believe me; I have never had such bad garlic bread.

"Show, show, let me try." Rimz snatches the bread out of my hands and takes a bite.

"Hmm, yaa, it is indeed, bad garlic bread."

"So that's it. You resigned and packed your stuff and walked out of the office?" Rishi asks. Things were still not making much sense to her.

"No actually not." I say taking another sip of my coffee, "After I submitted my resignation letter, I was called into the boss's office."

"And?" Rishi asks

"And they told me that my resignation had not been accepted."

"Ok. Then?"

"Then what? I asked them why."

"And?"

"And I was again given a lecture about my unawareness, about my environmental sensitivities and how that could help me and the firm, me and the environment if I worked with them."

"Hmm, needless to ask what happened next."

"Yeah, I insisted on resigning anyway."

"Hmm, they know you will be big trouble if you go out there all determined to stop them." Then she trails off into silence. "I don't know yaar," she says "… you are so lucky to be able to do what you feel like doing. You didn't need that job that badly. I am literally in a middle of a crisis here! I mean how am I going to get a house, and furnish it all when I have *no* job?"

"Yes, you are right. Life is unfair. I mean look at me; I am in a bigger crisis!" Rimz says taking out a huge bundle of papers out of her bag.

"What are these?" I ask.

"These are my BILLS! My telephone and credit card bills." She bursts out.

"Hmm, I always told you not to have four telephone connections. But what is the rest of this pile?"

"These are my credit card bills." She cries.

"My God! How many do you have?" Rishi asks as she leafs through the bundle.

"Twelve." Rimz looks almost in tears.

"What?" I almost choke on my coffee "Why the hell would you have twelve credit cards?"

"Because it sounded cool…then."

"What?" Rishi asks. She looks as shocked to hear that as I.

"Because it sounded cool", she repeats taking out a handkerchief to blow her nose. "It sounds cool when I say I have twelve credit cards." And after a little pause, she says, "If Rebecca Bloomwood from *Confessions of a Shopaholic* can do it then, why can't I?

"Oh of course you can. Go right ahead. But don't forget what happens to her." Amit says

"Oh you mean finding her true, hunky, and gorgeous love?" Rimz says batting her eyelashes.

"NO! More like her whole life gets turned upside down," Amit yells out as he gently slaps Rimz on the back of her head.

"Ugh! You are such a dream wrecker Amit."

"God Rimz, you could have just told everyone that, and not actually have got twelve credit cards. God!" Rishi says.

"This is so unfair!" I can't believe this; Rimz is actually in tears now. "First we like clothes and bags and shoes! And then we have to buy those! And then we have to work and earn money and PAY THESE BILLS!!!!! . It is so unfair!"

Most people are beginning to turn around by now to look at what is happening. But its no shocker. This generally happens when Rimz is with us.

"Rimz, calm down," Rishi says. "It's all going to be fine."

"I know," she says wiping her tears, "I know, I am going to leave for Kolkata tomorrow, and I am going to get selected and then, become the greatest pop sensation, and everything is going to be just fine."

"Yes..." Rishi says as she shooting me a look, unsure of what to say next.

"And I am really happy to see Amit's environmental concerns as well. It's going to be so much easier to take him to all the Page 3 parties when he becomes an environmentalist." Rima says as she put her handkerchief back in her bag. "And that reminds me, what about the book that you will be writing Rishi? I am going to Calcutta, and the Calcutta Book fair will be on then. I am sure I can use my charms to get a publisher for you."

"Yes, sure." Rishi says half smiling.

"Have you finalized the subject that you want to write on?" I ask.

"Oh! I know!" Rimz bursts out all excited by now. "You should write something really cool and different – like the story of a girl who gets married and goes to this new house and discovers that her mother-in-law is a witch! ... Or better still that her husband is a vampire. And she also becomes one later and... then something happens. Vampire stories are so in these days. Twilight simply rocks."

"No," Rishi interrupts her, "I know what I am going to write on. My write up will explore the rising rate of dysfunctional relationships." She says as she falls back in her chair letting out a sigh.

"God! Just look at us!" I say, "What is wrong with us? How old are we? 23? ...24?" I stammer as I look at Rishi – she is the oldest of us all. "We should be bursting with energy. We should be ... at the top of the world. Full of ideas. That is how strong the power of youth is. And instead we feel all sloppy and... drained and... old!"

"Hey" Rimz interrupts, "I don't know about you guys but I am *not* old. I am young. I am a pop queen."

"Yes, I am not old either" Rishi puts in.

"Yes... and... neither am I." I stutter. "And I am going to stop those people from destroying the habitat of those birds. And..." I continue, "And I need to find a job."

"Yes, that's what we all need." Rishi and Rimz say in unison.

Amit – The desire of being different – the desire to watch a movie being stronger than the will to pay a phone bill.

Why? Why? Why? Why the hell am I so different? Why can't I be just like other… normal people? Why can't I blindly and robotically work and focus on earning money and … invest it in suitable places so that they multiply and I can become more… rich? Oh God! What am I going to do? Just look at me! I have not bathed in two days. I have not shaved in four days. I have not washed the dishes since ·I don't know when. I AM SO COMPLETELY GOING INTO DEPRESSION! No! No! I must not let that happen. I must gather courage to… pull myself out of it. I am different, my conscience is not dead like that of the others and it is a great asset. That itself makes me a star…like … the North Star, which people look up to… and use to… identify directions. But right now I feel so low and … discouraged and … wrecked. How am I going to reach up there and become a star? Hmm, maybe I should go and watch a movie. A nice cheerful and feel-good one, with grinning dancers and happy weddings and unrealistically good-looking actors. Yes! And then start working. YES!

*Rishika – what do you do when you
lose a job? (You find another job.
That is what you do.)*

With my morning tea and breakfast laid on the dining table, I sit poring over the classifieds section in the newspaper. I could never have imagined even in my wildest dreams that *I, Rishika Malhotra*, would one day get fired, and be forced to go through the newspapers. No, not to read the news, but look for a job. I had a terrific academic record and an outstanding performance as a professional. And never, ever had I dreamt that in spite of going through the classifieds every single day, and uploading my CV on every job search website known. I would still not get a single, suitable option.

Most of the openings are for sales executives! None suit my profile. Then, I come across one ad.

Improve your English!!
Full package to learn other languages also.
Contact – 999666777

I take a deep breath and pick up my phone and call Amit.

"Hello." He replies.

"Hello."

"Hey, what happened?"

"Nothing *yaar*. There is no job. There is just no job that I can apply for."

"Hmm. No *yaar*. That can't be. Give it some time. There *has* to be a job."

"Hmm. Anyway, I found an ad that said 'improve your language'.

I am thinking of getting enrolled for the classes. It would help me improve my linguistic and writing skills."

"Yes, good idea. You should do that."

What the hell is the matter with him! Why is he so distracted? Is he even listening to what I am saying? I am in this great crisis here and all he has to say is hmm, ya, good idea?

"Amit, what is wrong with you? Why the hell are you sounding so distracted?"

"… I was… buying a movie ticket…"

Yeah. That explains it.

"God! You would never change. What happened to your money saving plan? The pending phone bill? Anyway. Talk to you later. Bye."

"Bye." He says with a smile.

Amit – He saves the world! (Well, he plans to)

Alright! Have seen a nice movie. Had a great time. Now must get back to work. I saw *Jab We Met* by the way and it is *really* cool. It is about young people falling in love. By the way, my holiday next year will include the places *Ratlam* and *Bhatinda*.

Anyway, we have a file here. I am going to dedicate it to the bird saving project and I will label it… yes, '*Save The Bird Land*'.

Yes, now…

Basic plan of action (basic P.O.A. – methodology)

Make a detailed P.O.A.:

↓

Follow the detailed P.O.A.

↓

Achieve satisfying and fulfilling results.

Yes, this looks good. Now let's detail it out.

The detailed P.O.A

Do the basic research on the foreign bird. (Google it)

Prepare a project report stating the need to save the land. (Do not complicate the task; just simply use Microsoft word to make the repost)

Take the repost to the animal saving authorities.

↓

Get the project approved.

↓

Get a saintly feeling for saving the foreign bird land!!!

Yes, this looks good.

Great! Now that half of the work is done, I can chill.

Rimz – when God closes a door, he opens a closet full of goodies.

Oh great! The reservation charts are here. Ok, let me see; coach no. C-4. Hmm, is there any M-20 or M-25 or any M in that range in the coach? Oh! WOW! One M-24.!!!!! Shekhar Verma. Cool. Ok, now let me see if my WL - 12 has been confirmed or not. Hey, it is confirmed!!!! AAAAAAh! And it's B-42. Right next to Shekhar's B-41.!!!! I am going to have a great journey.

I pick up my entire luggage and climb into the train.

I do not feel very good about this whole thing. Not the bit about going to Kolkata and becoming a superstar, but the part where I have to keep asking Dad to lend me money even for this trip! But its ok, I am going to be very rich, very soon. And then I am the one who is going to support the whole family. Anyway, where are the seats? B-41, B-41, …where is it? Oh! There it is. WOW!!!! It's a *Jab We Met* seat!!!! . And there is B-42 – my seat. Right opposite Shekhar's. But where is he?

I start pushing my luggage under the seat. Just then I notice a pair of legs pass me by and stop at the seat opposite. I maintain my calm, raise my head gracefully and pass a breezy smile. He smiles back.

Oh my God, My heart just skips a beat. Is he handsome or what? Thick curly black hair. Fair complexion. Deep, thoughtful and enigmatic eyes. Square jaw. Oh my God! I am in love.

⌒

Oh my God! He looks just like Brad Pitt!!! . And he has been looking at me smiling too. I must break the ice. I must make the first move. I know guys find it hot these days.

"Do you know who you resemble?" I ask him, as my hair billows in the breeze coming in from the window.

"No" he says as he flashes a dashing smile.

"You should figure that out." I say with an enigmatic smile. Ok, this is where I am supposed to act all mysterious and … be the mystery woman. I should get up most sensuously and leave. Just go… somewhere. I get up and start walking. Hmm, maybe I should go and stand near the door or something, and look at the landscape, just like they show in the movies. I am sure he will follow me there and then I can strike up a conversation. Yes. That is what I am going to do.

Ok, it's fifteen minutes since I came here and he is nowhere to be seen. I should go back, sit, and plan my next move.

I walk back to my seat and what do I see? Awww! He has fallen asleep. Oh! He sleeps like an angel. No wonder he didn't follow me. He just fell asleep. It's not that he is not interested in me.

Amit – A role reversal is on its way.

"Amit, I am in trouble."

It's Rishi on the phone. It's early in the morning and I am still half asleep.

"Why? What happened?"

"My parents just called. They have decided the date for the wedding."

"Oh! But you knew that right? You knew that it was going to be some time around in June, right?"

"Amit, I knew that it was going to be sometime in June. But I didn't know exactly when. There is a difference. Uh! You are *so* not helping."

"Ok, ok." I say as I sit up in my bed, trying to figure out what to say. "Ok. See. There is this guy you have been in love with for ... quite some time now, right?"

"Right."

"And you guys have been waiting to get married since like ... forever. Right?"

"Right."

"So if everything is right then what's wrong?"

"I don't know! Something ... somewhere ... just doesn't feel right. Right now I feel as if I have spoken to my parents under pressure. Iman and I, used to have a great time together in college. And it was wonderful how we both stated liking each other and how there was this ... strong mutual attraction, while we were on our college trip to Goa. But I feel that... " She trails off.

"Feel what Rishi?" I asked. This was quite a wake up call.

"I just feel that he was a different person back then. *I* was a different person back then. We used to sit and talk endlessly for hours. Remember that evening at Colva Beach? We both were sitting there, watching the sunset, and just talking; and we didn't realize that it was way past 12 in the night. And you had been sent to call us back. How mad Grover Sir had been at both of us !" And then she again falls silent.

"Yes, you both were inseparable. And I would never forget how you started ignoring me back then." I say.

"I know. And I am really sorry."

"Its ok. I understand. Although I didn't understand it that very well back then, but I do, now. But that is besides the point. Why do you feel that you both have become 'different people' now?" I ask.

"I don't know," she starts again, "Its just that … it seems that we no longer have any common interests. We just don't … do anything together. It's a different thing that now he is in Bangalore, but even when he was here, we never went out for movies. Now he thinks that it's a waste of time and he has so much of work to do. We never go out to dine anymore. I don't know Amit. It's not fun with him anymore. He has turned very … boring."

"I don't think it's a problem. I think it's just the work pressure. And it's a phase. And everything is going to be fine."

"If everything is going to be fine, then why is it that I can't feel that? And it's not just that he is boring. He just wants everything his way. And everything I do is wrong. Be it my driving, my cooking, the way I set up my room … *everything*."

"My God! You already sound like a married woman who is fed up with her husband." I joke.

"Shut up."

"I think you are worrying uselessly. And there is nothing as drastically wrong. Your imagination is working overtime."

"I don't know, I don't feel everything is fine. There is something wrong."

"I think there is nothing wrong, and you are simply, needlessly worrying about something that you should not even be thinking about now. Everyone has problems in their relationships. One just needs to work on it. There is nothing *wrong* anywhere. You just need a break. You need to … sit back and relax."

"Yeah. Like that is a possibility."

"Hmm, *vasay* what's the scene on the job front? Any luck?"

"No yaar."

"Ok and what happened to those English classes and that novel writing plan?"

"I am still to finalize the subject for the novel. And I have to go and check out the English classes today."

Rinz – lets do it, lets fall in love.

There are very few things I remember my teacher teaching me in school. And one of them is a quote from The Tempest. You know Shakespeare. And it goes something like this,

If the house is fair as this… nothing ill would dwell…

Ok, I don't remember it properly, but what it meant was that a man so handsome can't have anything evil about him. And looking at this devastatingly handsome face, I feel how true and intelligent people were even like four hundred years ago. I mean it's hard to imagine them any different than monkeys, but still they were *so* right. Oh! Look! He is beginning to move and is slowly opening his eyes. Wow!

"Hi" I look up. Oh my God! It's the Brad Pitt look alike!!!!! . He is talking to me!!!! "Hieee. You are … up."

"Yeah," he says taking a deep breath.

"Yeah." I giggle shyly.

"So, where to?" he asks.

"Oh me? I am going to audition for *Come On India! Sing and Dance!!!* In Kolkata."

As I say this, his expression changes to a person's who has just accidentally ingested cow dung.

There is an awkward smile on my face too. "And you? Where are you going?"

"To Kolkata. For the same."

Rishika – when students become teachers.

Things have been changing lately. I have never felt so stressed out before. I so desperately need a job, and I see not even a single ray of hope! And instead of going for a job interview, here I am, enrolling myself for language classes. And this place is not giving me the best feeling. The staircase I am climbing right now is just not helping matters. The building is so deserted and dilapidated that it is the fourth time I am actually killing the urge to turn around and run away. "I must not run away. I must stick to it. I must remember what my MBA friends always keep telling me – never give up and make as many contacts as you possibly can." Finally I reach the third floor and march into the empty corridor. And there it is – the place she is looking for. The signboard reads:

LANGUAGES FOR ALL
(YOUR FINAL DESTINATION TO LEARN ANY LANGUAGE AT ALL)

I take a deep breath and push open the door. There is a guy sitting in front of a table. He must be the receptionist. I walk over to him.

"Hi," I say with a smile.

"Hello." He replies.

"I had a word with you on the phone this morning." I say.

He looks back at me with a frown as he leans back slightly turning his head a little.

"I wanted to enroll for your English classes." I continue.

"Oho! You are Miss Rishika ji. Come, come, please, sit down." The guy says with a very heavy Haryanvi accent.

I smile and sit

"So you want to join our English class." He says with a smile.

"Yes."

"But why? I see you speak in English so good."

Ok, he works at a language school, and can't speak a single sentence in correct English. This really does not look like a good investment.

"May I know what your qualifications are?" he asks me.

Hey, wait a minute. Instead of taking classes here, why don't I …

I paste a smile on my face and say,

"Actually sir, I have a copy of my CV with me, if you would want to see."

"Show show, I would!" he says nodding with enthusiasm.

I hands her CV to him and he looks at it with concentration, narrowing his eyes behind his thick glasses.

"So you have got three articles published under your name."

"Yes sir." I smile.

"Very interesting this is. I am very impressed on your CV. Actually one of our teacher left the job tomorrow. We have a position open. If you want to come." He says

"That sounds good sir. What would be the job profile like?"

The guy looks at her frowning deeply again.

"I mean what all would I be… needed to doing here." I try to … explain in… his language.

"Oh nothing much. You would be teaching the students speaking English."

Amit – Now Rishika has a job and he doesn't. What should he do now?

"Cheers to your new job." I say as I raise my glass of strawberry iced tea.

"Cheers" Rishika says. It's evening and almost dark outside with heavy traffic on the roads. Everyone is heading home. Rishika and I are having our evening tea and coffee in our favorite coffee shop.

"You are one smart woman I must say. Went to enroll for their classes, and came back with a job." I say

"Oh please *yaar*. You should have seen the place! And the guy! My God! He could not speak one sentence correctly in English, and he is actually running a school of languages. Anyway, you tell me, how is your 'save the bird land' project getting on?"

"Hmm, I have a plan of action in place." I say. "And I think that things are going to … fall into place. Now I am worried about my finances. I have no money left at all."

"Hey," Rishika says as she sipping her coffee, "why don't you use that diploma in psychology. All those evening classes that Sehar forced you to take should pay off somewhere…better now than never." Rishika bursts out laughing.

"Hey. It's not the best time to pull my leg ok? The other day I got this huge telephone bill of mine. And that too because I had been talking to Sehar for hours on end, can you beat that?"

"No," she says, "but seriously, why can't you use that diploma? These days there is a huge demand for counselors in schools. I am sure you would get through somewhere if you try. God! I still remember the expression on your face when she used to drag you to those evening classes."

"Can we stop talking about her?"

"Ok, ok. Sorry. But seriously, you should try for such a job."

"Yeah. Maybe I should. By the way, any news from Rimz?" I ask

"Not as yet." She says.

Rimz – Joy, love and hope.

I get off the train and set foot on the platform – the Kolkata Railway Station. And I can just about feel the joy. The city is not called the *City Of Joy* for nothing. You set foot here and you can sense the happiness in the air. You can *feel it*. Everyone is smiling. And they are all so polite and… melodious. I don't understand a word they say but it still sounds so pleasant. Bengali is indeed a sweet language. Even the sound of the bell before and after the announcements is melodious; it has kind of a sweet musical touch to it. It is different then anything I have ever heard at any other railway station. And the people here are so sweet. I have walked only like some ten steps, and worried people are already requesting me to check if their name is on the reservation list or if they had bought the ticket to the right destination. It's so nice to help people – to do something for a cause.

Hmm, ok, lets see, its 8 A.M. the auditions start tomorrow morning at 10. So I have the whole day with me. I should go and check into a hotel and then head to the book fair and look for a publisher for Rishi. Yes! I should do that.

Amit – He is hungry but Rishi just won't let him eat.

There comes a time in your life when you see everything happening around you and you feel that all of this, and only this, makes complete sense. This is so much *not* like that moment. I quit my job during the recession. I am struggling to save the land that rightfully belongs to some migratory birds. And I have taken up a job in a *school* as a counselor to… help children deal with their issues as they grow up! I mean how unpredictable can life get? Anyway, the interview was a piece of cake. If you really ask me, they would have hired anyone. Anyone who was willing to sit in a room and talk to children about the problems they thought they were facing. I am on my way back home after the interview. Its mid-day and I am starving. I think I will go to some nice eating joint and have something to eat first. A pizza sounds nice. Yeah, *Dominos*. But wait! I can't afford that, not just yet anyway. I lost my job. No, no, no! No *Dominos*, I should go to *McDonald's*. Yes, that will be cheaper and affordable. Yeah I should accept the situation - my financial crisis and eat at *McDonald's*. I enter the mall, push the glass door open, walk to the counter and place my order.

"Two Vegetarian Surprise. One coke, one paneer salsa wrap and one large fries."

"Would you like to take our combo sir? You would save ..." I cut the guy at the counter immediately.

"Yes. Combo, it will be. Save, I should." I almost shout and then realize that I am garnering too much attention and lower my voice.

"Sure sir." The guy punches some keys on the machine. These people, they are really trained hard to never react. It is truly amazing.

"Would that be all sir?" he asks me.

"Hmm, yeah. That should be enough."

"Would you like to have it here or take away sir?"

"I will have it here."

He nods and I step aside so that the other people can place their orders. That is when my phone starts ringing. I look at the screen, it is Rishi.

"Hi!" I say cheerfully.

"Amit, I want you to come to my place right now!"

"Ok, is everything alright?"

"Can you for once just do as I say and not ask any questions!" she sounds mad.

"Ok, ok! Chill. I am coming."

She hangs up the phone "Excuse me; make it a take away please." I say to the guy behind the counter.

Rimy – She feels like a lost tourist in a foreign land.

Hmm, it is huge indeed! I have been roaming around for an hour (alone). And each and every being is talking in Bengali, and I don't understand a word of it. Anyway, it's enormous. And I have been walking, and walking, and walking. I need FOOD. I am thirsty and famished. I wander around in search of food. *But food is nowhere to be found.* We have books, books, books, and more books. BUT NO FOOD!!!! Where's the food? One can't *eat* books you know. I go on walking as the path bends around the staggered stalls and halls. AND WHAT DO I SEE???!! *PARADISE*!!!!!!! IT'S A *FOOD BAZAR*!!!!! PEPSI AND LIPTON!!!! THEY ARE ALL THERE!!! Suddenly I feel like one of those lost travelers, trudging through the desert and chancing upon an oasis. I immediately buy a half liter bottle of *Mountain Dew. Thakavat ke agey jeet hai.* I sip the drink and … oh! It is so refreshing. I pay with a 20-rupee note and a 2-rupee coin. The vendor looks at me and says "Twenty five." I frown at him and start searching for the printed price on the bottle. "Twenty five." He says again. The printed price is nowhere to be found on the bottle and he knows it. Anyway, it is just a matter of three rupees – it's ok! I give him three rupees more and move on in search of food. I sniff a familiar aroma in the air. It is tickling my brain. What is it? Oh yes! It is fish! I dash towards the food stall and go through the rate list.

Fish Roll ------------------- Rs 25

Fish Chop ------------------- Rs 20

Egg Roll ------------------- Rs 15

Chicken Roll------------------ Rs. 30

Mutton Roll ------------------ Rs 25

(It is a long list)

Hmm, cheap food indeed! But wait a minute. I observe the stall critically. It does not look very hygienic. I force myself to move ahead. What do I see at a distance? A NESCAFE STALL. Oh God! Please let there be Maggi. Please, please, please! I move to the stall and see the Maggi Cuppa noodles stocked on the shelf.. Hmm, not bad. Let's have it.

"One Cuppa Mania." I tell the guy at the counter.

And he says something that sounds like *asta bhasta* in Bengali.

I look at him blankly and slowly ask him in Hindi, "*Kitna hua?*"

And he again says something that sounds like *bhasta bhasta*.

I ask very slowly in English this time, "how much money? …One Cuppa Noodles?"

And *asta bhasta* is what I get again.

I shake my head as he says something holding two cups of noodles in his hands.

"No, no. one, I want one. *hume ek chahiye.*" I say with all the hand gestures. God! I so understand what all the foreigners must feel like when they have to converse with the local people who don't understand their language.

"He is saying that we have one free with one. Would you like to get both of them made right now or would you bring the other one later and get it made then?"

Ok, it's a guy's voice from behind me.

I turn around with flair and I see a guy dressed in a *kurta* and a pair of blue jeans. Oh! So that is what *asta bhasta* means.

"Oh" I say as I look at the guys, "one now, the other later." I say to the guy behind the counter as I turn back to him. I don't know why our brain starts sending signals to the mouth to talk in English when the eyes can see that the person in front does not know the language.

The guy behind the counter repeats his *lasta fasta* to the cute tall guy in the *kurta*, and I am given one cup of noodles with hot water in it, and another completely dry.

I turn around and look at the guy and am just about to ask him the amount when he smiles and says "Twenty rupees."

"Ok. Thank you." I say as I hand over the money. "Thank you, thank you so much." I repeat myself. Now I know why all the foreigners I have helped in all the shops always thank me thrice. I walk away with my steaming cup of noodles and I again observe that each and every person is talking in Bengali. And I don't understand a thing! It's a queer feeling – hearing everyone talk and not understand a word of what they are saying. I cannot understand what that couple sitting over there is saying. I cannot understand what that old man is jabbering about with the middle aged man. And I cannot understand what the woman is screaming about or why the three children are running away from her. I don't even understand what this small doggie is thinking as he comes towards me. AAAAAh! And I don't understand why he is holding my jeans with his teeth and growling like that. AAAAAAh! I shut my eyes tight and scream.

"He wants your noodles." I hear someone saying as I suddenly stop screaming. I open my eyes and see the same guy who helped me with the noodles. Can he read my mind or what?

He shoos the dog away and says, "Hi again."

"Oh! Thank you so much. I mean, hi. ... sorry!" I say all confused as I check my jeans. Damn! That dog has made three holes in my jeans!

"My name is Vikrum Ghosh." He says as he stands up after shooing the dog away.

"I am Rimz." I say smiling gracefully at him.

"It's nice to meet you... again. What do you do?"

"I am a pop singer." I nod earnestly, setting my hair. "What do you do?" I ask him.

"I am a student. But I am here for a few months to help my dad with his business."

"Oh, what business?" I ask.

"He runs a publishing house." He says casually as I almost choke on my Cuppa Mania.

"Are you ok?" he asks with genuine concern as I start to cough, "Should I get water for you?"

"Yes. I mean no! I am fine. Thanks."

"I am sorry, but what did you tell me your name was?"

"Rimz, no! Rishika. My name is Rishika."

"Ok... Rishika" he says with some amount of suspicion – a semi confused frown accompanied by a smile.

"You know something Vikrum," I say clearing my throat, "I feel like I have been roaming around this place like forever now. And I keep seeing that interesting building across the road. I have heard it's called Science City. I would love it if you would accompany me there." I have to make friends with him before I tell him that *I, Rishika*, am writing a novel, and wish to get it published. I have to lie. *But I must do it.*

"Sounds good to me," he says.

"Great then! Let's go!"

And then we go roaming around Science City. I see a board and exclaim, "Hey! Evaluation hall. Sounds interesting. Let's go there." I wonder what they would evaluate there? Our beauty? Our mind? … What? He smiles back at me and says, "It's not the evaluation hall, it's the evolution hall."

"Yeah, yeah. That is what I meant. Let's go there."

God! Huge creatures there were all those millions of years ago. A four-foot big scorpion. Can you beat that? And those stupid, moving fake animals. I am scared and I don't know how many times I have clung to Vikrum's sleeve. And then we enter the mirror maze. I am lost in it. And Vikrum comes to find me. We visit the huge hall where they have all those games and toy thingies next. There is something using which you can not only generate a mini tornado but also touch it. But the best part is the walk-on piano. Vikrum and I play that for a long time and have so much fun. We play so many tunes, "Ha ha ha." I throw my head back and laugh. Such fun.

"You know, it was such fun hanging out with you." I say. I cannot realize it but there is a genuine honesty in my voice.

"Me too." He says with the sweetest smile ever.

"You know, I hate to bring it up like this … especially after all the time we have spent together, I really don't want you to think that, that was the reason why I wanted to hang out with you, but, I am writing a novel and I am … looking for a publisher…" I say hesitantly and not too sure as to how to put it across.

"Hey. There is nothing to feel sorry about. In fact you could have told me earlier. We are looking for young authors. In fact, that is what I have come here for." he says sounding hugely interested.

"Really! You mean I can forward you the manuscript?" I ask wide eyed.

"Sure" he says handing me his card. "Oh, But there is a problem. I am returning to Australia next week. But don't worry. I will tell Dad about you. There won't be any problem."

"Thanks. You are such a darling." I say

"No problem. You are a very interesting and a fun loving person. I am sure your work is going to be just like that as well."

I smile. Oh my God! Am I blushing?

And then we sit down to a nice long chat as the sun sets, turning the sky blue, yellow and then orange before the final dark inky blue hue.

Amit – He does not really get it why Rishi is so upset these days.

I should have packed more food. I am sure Rishi has not had any lunch cooked at her place and now I will have to share my take away. It is hardly enough for me. As it is I ordered only *two* Veg. Surprise instead of my regular *three*.

I stand in front of the door and ring the bell.

Rishi opens the door, turns around and walks off.

"Amit, the wedding is off." She says walking ahead.

"WHAT? No wait, I heard something else. What did you say?"

"Amit, I said THE WEDDING IS OFF. THERE IS GOING TO BE NO WEDDING! IS THAT TOO HARD FOR YOU TO

UNDERSTAND?"

"No… I mean … ok… but…"

"BUT WHAT?"

"But… why are you … thinking like this?" I stammer.

"Because I hate him! And I am not going to talk to him again. EVER."

"Rishi, calm down. Here, have something to eat." I offer her the stuff in the brown paper bag.

"What have you got?" she grabs the bag from my hands.

"Some… stuff."

"Good. I was very hungry." She opens up the paneer salsa wrap and takes a bite. I was thinking of sharing it. Anyway, I will have another… some other time.

"What happened?" I ask.

"Nothing." She says as she chews on the wrap.

I give her a questioning look.

"Iman's a jerk, that's all."

"And why is that?"

"His priorities are all screwed up."

"Priorities?" I ask, confused.

"Yes, we have been looking for a house. I finally selected one from the ones we short listed and asked him to come over this weekend and he refused and said that I could see and take the decision."

"So?" I ask.

"So? It blew into a huge fight. No Amit, really, if he doesn't even have time to come and see the house that we are going to live in, I really don't want to marry him."

103

"Rishi?"

"What? Don't you start *Rishi-ing* me now."

"Ok, if the fight was just over this thing then I would say that you are over reacting. But if there is something else, then tell me. I am sure it can be sorted out."

"It's just that…" she takes a deep breath, "… I feel that he has … changed. He feels like a completely different person now. His job… doesn't give him any time at all to talk to me. And …" she trails off into silence.

"And what?"

"And whenever we talk now… we end up fighting. I don't want to get married if this is how things are going to be." she says taking a sip of the Coke.

"Hmm. So that is what it is, you are scared."

She gives a puppy faced look.

"It's ok. Everything is going to be fine. See the problem is in the situation and not with him or you. You are struggling here, finding a job and trying to save money. And he is slogging it out there to earn. And then, both of you have expectations, which are not being fulfilled. So just understand that and talk to him."

"But he…"

"No buts. Just pick up the phone and call him."

"But he screamed at me."

"And you didn't? And as far as I know, you must have been the one to start it."

"Here now, take the phone and call him."

She takes the phone to dial Iman's number as I take the paneer salsa wrap from her hand.

Just then the phone starts to ring.

"Oh! It's Rimz!" she says.

"Hi!" she says as she receives the call.

"Rishi!!!! I have the greatest news for you!!!! . I found a publisher for you!!!!" She is literally shouting with joy. I can actually hear her from 4 feet away from the phone.

Rimz – She is in a big auditorium now.

"All enrolled candidates can proceed to room number eleven to collect their ID cards." Ok, so this is all high-tech. They are making the announcement and I can't even make out where the voice is coming from – no speakers are visible. And I must say there are so many people who have just come here and don't have any kind of talent whatsoever. God! People are so disillusionalized in life. Anyway, so room number eleven is where I need to go.

Room number eleven looks good. It's not that small, and a table is neatly set in front of a bright red, nicely designed backdrop that says '*Come On India! Sing and Dance!!*' There is only one guy, who is collecting his ID card from the table, and I must tell you, he is just *not* good looking. He is not very tall, and his complexion is as dark as his curly, black hair. He is so skinny that it looks like God has forgotten to put flesh on him – he is all bones. I can simply blow him out of my way. I reach the table and he turns and guess what? He bumps into me. Foolish moron!

"Oh! I am sorry," he says. Oh god! He sounds like such a *gawar*.

"It's ok; just get out of my way." I say, trying not to meet his eyes.

"I am Kamal, from Ropar, Punjab." Hmm, no wonder.

"And I am Rimz, with a 'zee', from Delhi. Now if you'll excuse me."

"Oh! Sorry," he smiles. Uh! Even his smile is hideous.

"We are next to each other for this contest. It was nice meeting you." he says and walks away.

Oh damn!

Part Three

Amit – Does he really think he can handle out of control, impish kinds?

O k! So this is what it is like. My first day at school. I mean … job, it is my first day at my job (in the school) and I have been asked to go to each class and … get friendly with students. And I will have to start with standard III B. Hmm, so how tough can it be? I am sure it will be child's play.

Ok, so here we are. Everything is in place – the teacher's table, the chair, the blackboard, the door, the windows … Oh come on! These are children, not some aggressive prisoners in a jail! I decide that I will have to stay calm, not think too much and just … do what I am supposed to do. I keep my cell phone (which is literally falling apart) on the table, turn to the black board, and write my name. Isn't that what I am supposed to do? At least that is what they show in all those high school drama shows and movies, isn't it?

"My name is Amit Trehan. And I am your new counselor."

They look at me blankly. They seem to be as clueless as to who and what I am supposed to be. Or am I?

I fumble for a few seconds and then say, "I am here to solve your problems. So if you have any kind of problems, you can, without hesitation come to me."

Ok, now I fall quiet, unsure of how to proceed. So I just walk the width of the classroom and then sit on the chair. That is when one boy raises his hand.

"Yes." I say, "What is your name?"

"Sarit, sir."

"Yes Sarit."

"There is a sum in our math book. Exercise no 12.1. I am not able to solve it."

Oh no! They have got me completely wrong. How can I solve their math problems? I have barely passed the subject myself. I secured 36 ½ in math in my 12th board exams. I try to smile and retain that calm look, but it is difficult.

"I didn't mean *these* problems. I meant if you have any kind of personal problems. Like … if your friend hurt you …or… you had a fight with someone…"

I see another hand shoot up.

"Yes please."

"Sir in the Hindi Period, Rohit hit me on my head with my pencil box," a girl says as if she is almost going to break into tears.

Oh no! Now how can I explain that I don't mean physical hurt? I mean… hey! Wait a minute! A kid getting beaten by another kid? That is my case. I mean…this is a case for me. I should try to help and … prevent the aggressor from hitting other kids. YES.

"Where is Rohit?" I ask scanning the class expecting him to stand up.

A short boy stands up. He has an unpleasant frown on his forehead.

"Hello Rohit. How are you?" I ask sounding as friendly as I possibly as I could.

"I am fine," he says as if I have asked him the most offensive question.

"Is it true that you hit that girl with her pencil box?" I ask

"No." he says

"No sir he is lying. He hit me. Here," she says pointing at her forehead.

Ok, it isn't going to work like this. I will have to talk to them in private.

"What is your name?" I ask the girl.

"Shikha, sir."

"Shikha I want to see you in my office during recess today. Ok?"

"Ok sir." She nods most obediently and sits down.

Hmm, we have fallen silent again. Now what am I supposed to do? We still have a full thirty-five minutes to go. Oh! I know!!! . The most obvious trick that every teacher resorts to when he does not know what to do.

"Alright!" I say brightly, "Now all of you tell me your name and the name of your favorite subject. Let's start with you." I say as I approach the boy sitting on the front bench in the first row.

"Good morning sir. My name is Kiran and my favorite subject is science."

"Very good. Kiran. And why is science your favorite subject?"

Great! Its working! There are some really talkative kids. They can go on and on when they start talking about themselves. Anyway, the bell has rung – the period is over. And I have to leave now.

"Ok children. It was really nice talking to you all. I will see you all next week, unless you want to come and discuss something. Except you, Shikha. I want to see you during the recess today."

"Yes sir." She replies.

Great! I get up to leave the classroom. I turn around when I suddenly remember – my cell phone. Stupid of me! I was going to forget it on the table. I turn around again and go to the table.

WHAT! I CELL PHONE IS NOT THERE!!! I keep staring there for a few seconds in shock. And then I frantically search my pockets – it is not there either. I look under the table – it is not there.

"Did anyone see my cell phone?" I ask the class.

All of them look at me blankly (again.)

Great!

Rimy – She knows she and Shekhar and gonna go a long way. (Yes, she just knows that)

We all have submitted the video clips that feature our best talents and have been asked to wait in this hall. Everyone is here. Even Shekhar (!!!!!) He looks very dashing and completely hot with the guitar in his hands. Its evening now and we have been waiting here, sitting – doing nothing. But, I am smart. I have utilized my time well, I have done a little research, and I have come to know that Shekhar has come here with a childhood friend of his. Both are completely inseparable. The friend's name is Ravi. I am now sitting right opposite them, staring the whole time. Actually Shekhar does not look like Brad Pitt; he looks more like Robert Redford (when he was young of course, like in *Barefoot in the Park*). Well, there is this chic female who has just entered the hall with some papers in her hand.

"All right everyone, the judges have gone through your video clips and we have the final fifty here." She announces

No one in the hall utters a word or moves a muscle – everyone is so tense.

"And the names are…"

Oh my God! Oh my God!!!! ! Please let Shekhar be in!!!! ! Please let Shekhar be in!!!! !

"…Vishwas, Jimmy, Kunal, Vimal…"

She goes on rambling names and after some thirty random names she says, "…Shekhar, Ravi…"

Oh! Thank God! What a relief!

And after some forty more names, I hear it – "Rimz and Kamal…"

Wow! Great! We are already being paired.

After announcing all the names the girl says "All these people please follow me, the judges want to have a word with you. And the rest …can leave. I wish them the best of luck for all their future endeavors."

It is an intimidating auditorium. The ceiling is so high it seems to touch the sky. A number of seats fill the whole space. And at the end is this grand stage. And on that stage sit those three judges in whose hands lay our fates. The judges are familiar – Mannu Salik, Naved Bukhtawar and Ranisha Sunoy. This is the first time it actually hits me. I have made it! I have made it to the final fifty.

"Welcome everyone," says Mannu Salik from the stage "welcome to a new beginning." "We have gone through the video clips that you submitted, and I must say all of you rock. If it were in my hands, I would have made all of you the winners. Sadly that cannot be."

Oh my God! He is looking at me as he speaks! And he is smiling. Oh God! I am blushing now.

"It's ok Mannu, stop flirting with the children," Ranisha Sunoy says, "and tell them what they have to do next."

"As you say princess," Mannu says and again turns to us. "We will have the first round three days from now, for which, each one of you will have to prepare a song that has been sung by a singer of your choice."

We all listen to him quietly as the other two judges scan the crowd with their hawk like, fixed expressions. Huh, I don't know about the rest, but I am very clear whose song I will choose.

Amit – He just does not like children. (Well, not all of them)

Alright. Half of the day's work is done. I have managed to visit four classes and it is lunchtime now, and the lunch from the canteen is already here. Great! I sit down and am about to uncover the lunch that has been sent when I hear,

"May I come in sir?"

I look up to see a young girl standing at the door with a tiffin box in her hands. Oh! It is Shikha from class III B.

"Oh yes! Come, come!"

She walks timidly and sits on the chair in front of my table.

"You've had your lunch?"

"No sir."

"Oh good! Then we can have lunch together! Show me, what have you got?"

She keeps her tiffin box on the table and opens it. It is *aloo ke paranthe* with mango pickle. WOW!

"So tell me, what happened in the classroom?"

"Rohit is a thief, Sir."

"Is it?"

"Yes Sir. He always steals. He steals from everyone. Today he stole the new pencil that my *Mamu* had got for me from America. I saw him taking it out of my pencil box. And when I asked him to give it back to me, he said he didn't have it. And when I said that he was lying and that I had seen him taking it, then he hit me on my head with the pencil box."

Oh! Poor thing. "Hmm. That is very bad of him." It's ok, kids do things like these. They just need to be taught right.

"And Sir, he also stole your cell phone. I saw him doing that."

What! He is such a #@$$%^&!!!!

"Oh no! Really? But why didn't anyone tell me when I asked?"

"Because everyone is scared of him, Sir. If anyone opposes him, he beats them up at recess. After you left he also made fun of you and said that you had a broken Mobile phone and you were very poor, and even his servants had better phones then yours."

WHAT!!!! HE IS SUCH A ... I AM GOING TO TELL HIS PARENTS THAT!!!!!

Rimz – It's a new place, new friends, and new irritating elements.

We are all here and awaiting our turn to go on stage and sing. I am well prepared, and today I feel that no one can beat me; I know that. But there's a long time before I go on stage. I am number 34, and Shekhar is number 22. I really wonder whose song he is going to sing.

So as I sit here doing nothing, I might as well tell you what the place is like. First of all, it's a *huge* complex. There is this huge auditorium that I told you about last time, and right next to it is this huge stadium, where they say they are going to conduct all the outdoor events. And behind the auditorium are the nice cozy cottages that we are staying in. Each cottage has these two rooms. And the girl sharing my cottage is Natasha. She is from Bangalore, has thin, long legs and wears sleazy clothes. But anyway, how does that matter? I know she is not going to last. I have made a tiny little chart in which I have listed all the contestants and I am going to strike off their names as they get eliminated. And I know the day is not far when I am going to strike off Natasha's name. Yeah, so what was I saying? About the place, right…all meals are served in the stadium. It's kind of nice to have dinner outside in the open. A really cool breeze blows and creates a wonderfully romantic atmosphere, which, one day I am going to use to confess my feelings for Shekhar. Oh! Contestant number 19 has gone on stage (which is Natasha, by the way). Let's see, what she sings in the tight, skin-fit white dress with a loose hood. Ah! What is she going to sing? The dress is so tight, she can hardly breathe.

Hmm, so she is singing Kylie's '*How Do You Feel In My Arms*' hmm, she is not all that bad. And it's not just me who seems to be thinking like that. The judges also seem to like her a lot. In fact, Ranisha Sunoy gives her a standing ovation and tells the rest of us, "You guys have some competition."

But the rest of the contestants till contestant number 22 pretty much suck. Contestant number 22 (who is Shekhar by the way) rocks. He sings Jason Mraz's '*I am gonna make it all mine*" and by God, he is not just a good singer but an excellent dancer as well. All the three judges seem to love him, and why won't they? He is *so good*. Contestant number 23, Ravi sings some old Bryan Adams song but the judges like him too for some weird reason.

Hmm, finally its contestant number 33 – Kamal from the village. And guess whose song he is singing? Kishore Kumar –

> '*Tera muj se hai pehle ka nata koi,*
> *yuhi nahi dil lubhata koi,*
> *jane tu ya jane naa.*'

Uh! What a *gawar* he is. But surprisingly, the judges like him too. All three of them can't stop praising him, and place him on cloud number nine. Uh! God! Anyway, it's my turn to dazzle them with magic now.

I step up on the stage in my black and white striped slacks and the black and red long top. I can feel all eyes on me. I can sense everyone looking at my clothes and accessories. The colorful beads necklace and the bangles, my awesome recently permed hair…to tell you the truth, I quite felt I looked like Madonna, just then. I walk to the center of the stage and start singing –

'Like a virgin, touched for the very first time.'

I finish singing the song like a true diva. The judges look at me silently and all the other contestants start clapping. What does it mean?

Naved Bukhtawar says, "Rimz, that is your name right?"

"Yes sir." For the first time, he has uttered something. I am really getting jittery. Is he going to fire me? What will he say? He always wears a kurta. What if my performance is not culturally acceptable to him?

"You got the feelings and the emotions right. It was a very … passionate performance. But I think you need to work more on your singing."

Oh! Thank God! He is not firing me.

"I tend to differ a little in my opinion Naved ji" Mannu Salik says, "I think it was a strong performance. I think she sang pretty well."

"But at times pretty good is not good enough Mannu." Mr. Naved says

"Ok, what do you think Ranisha?" Mannu Salik says

She shrugs her shoulders and her face has that what-should-I-say expression.

"But you don't need to worry Rimz, your performance was definitely not bad. You are not getting eliminated in this round." As

Mannu Salik says this, Mr. Naved looks a little pissed off. Hmm. My first performance and I am already the reason for controversy. I *like* it!

Amit – He gets a new someone to have lunch with.

After Shikha and I finish our lunch, she leaves. I call up the office and ask for Rohit's contact number. I have to get in touch with his parents. I call up his home and a male voice answers the phone.

"Hello, can I talk to …Rohit's mother please?" I say

"She does not live here." The voice answers sternly. Hmm, strange.

"Ok, can I talk to his father then?"

"I am sorry but he is busy. He can't take any calls right now."

Hmm.

"Ok, would you please tell him that Amit called from Rohit's school and had a very urgent matter to discuss? I would want to meet him as soon as possible." And I have not even finished when the call is terminated.

"Hello? Hello?" there is no reply.

Rimy – is again all set to confess her love.

Tonight is the night, when I shall confess my love for Shekhar. I am sitting in the stadium all awash in the silvery moonlight. It's a clear night with cool breeze that is tenderly tickling my neck. Dinner will be served in ten minutes, and just like every day, Shekhar will come exactly seven minutes after it has been served. We have all been preparing for the next round and just as expected, sleazy Natasha has been flirting with Shekhar. But the truth is she stands no chance in front of me. I sit and observe everyone around me. It has been five days since we arrived and I can already see small groups getting formed. Some guys are trying to hit on the girls and some girls are trying to hit on some guys – the usual scenario. As to the next round, it will be *'either dance or play a musical instrument'* round. I am really excited about it since we can team up with someone or go ahead with a solo. I want to talk to Shekhar about this too – ask him if he will be my partner. Ok, they are serving dinner. I take out my sipper from my bag and take a sip when I hear someone say,

"Hi," uff! It's Kamal.

"Hi," I say flatly.

"I was thinking of asking you if you would perform with me in the next round."

"Oh no! Actually Shekhar and I will be performing together. So… maybe next time?" I say cheerfully. "Oh! There he is." Shekhar is finally here. "I am sorry but I have to go right now. I will catch you later." Uff!! Thank God, Shekhar is here. Or I would have been stuck with Kamal! And he is asking me to perform with him. Can you beat that?

"Ok, not a problem, catch you later." He says, flashing his stupid smile.

I go up to Shekhar and say, "Hi! How are you?" He is in the queue, waiting for his turn to serve himself. Hmm.

He looks at me chewing gum and says, "Hi, I am good, how are you?"

"I am good, I am … good."

"Great!"

There is an awkward silence.

We stand there as the queue moves ahead and finally we reach the buffet table. "So, what kind of food do you like?" I ask.

"All kinds. Yeah, all kinds."

"That is *so* cool!" I say as I giggle.

"Do you mind if I sit with you for dinner?" I ask as we walk away from the buffet table, our plates in our hands.

"Not at all!" he smiles again.

Yes! He *likes* me!

We go and sit on the steps. I start eating. But Shekhar takes out his cell phone and starts to type a message. Oh my God! He has a girl friend!!!! . And it is the daily 'I am going to have dinner now *jaan*' message!!!!! . Damn! Anyway, it's not a big deal for me to split them up. I am an expert at that you know. I wait for him to finish messaging and then I ask him,

"Shekhar, I was just thinking, how cool it would be if both of us performed together for the next round?"

"Actually…" he stammers, "I am performing with Ravi for the next round."

"Oh! It's ok," I let out a light casual laugh, "never mind. Next time." I say.

Just then his phone starts ringing. He looks at the screen and says, "Excuse me. I need to take this call." He gets up, picks up his plate and walks away. Uh! I am sure it's his dumb girlfriend. I sit there trying to figure out what I should start thinking now, should I –

"Would this pretty lady mind if I joined her for dinner?" Oh God! It's Kamal again!

"Not at all." I say making a face.

My eyes are still fixed on Shekhar, I see him joining Ravi and giving him a high five. I think I faintly heard him say, "Thank you so much dude!"

"So you know only Kishore Kumar songs, is it?" I ask as I put a spoonful of rice and curry in my mouth.

"No," he lets out a laugh, "why would you think so?"

"Just like that." I say casually.

"You sang Madonna's song. But that does not mean you know only Madonna's songs, right?"

THAT IS SOO NOT TRUE! IDIOT! "Yeah, that's ...not true." I say aloud.

"What are you and Shekhar planning to do for the next round?"

Oh no! What can I say? I cannot lie now.

"Actually I just had a word with him. I wanted to perform 'Material Girl' with him, but he didn't like the idea so much. So I will go solo now."

"Oh! Ok."

"So, is there any other singer you like besides Kishore Kumar? Someone from the western music world?"

"Yeah, I like Barry Manilow's songs."

"Ok, never heard of him."

"He maybe a little... outdated now. But I really love his songs. I listen to his songs and …I can feel what true love would actually be like." He sounds a little hesitant and shy as he says this, "His song '*I can't smile without you*' is my favorite song. If I make it to the finals that is the song I will sing."

Great! The only international singer he likes is an unknown oldie! Wonderful! What else can a *gawar* like him be fond of? But as he says this, I can see him dreaming away to glory. And I also feel a little touched; he is after all sharing his secret with me. I mean I will never tell anyone that I am going to sing '*Erotica*' if I make it to the finals. But wait a minute! Did he just say 'what true love *would* be like? Does that mean…

"Oh God! Have you never been in love?"

"…No… have you been…?" he stutters.

"*Thousands of times*!" I laugh cheerfully and then I realize I shouldn't be saying things like that to a complete stranger. It does not look … very good. "I mean… yes I have been…"

Silence.

"So you mean you have never liked any girl?"

"No."

"O my God! You like guys don't you!"

"*No*!"

"Oh my God!! You are blushing!"

"No I am not,"

"Yes you are."

"No I am not. And I did like a girl once. It's just that I don't start telling people about my personal life in the first meeting."

"Kamal, you and I, we both know it's not our first meeting."

"Ok."

"What ok? Tell me about her."

"I was in the eighth standard. Her name was Priyanka," I can see him blushing again; looking down shyly at the ground "she was our class teacher's daughter. So I never…"

"Oh no! That is so sad. But I can see you remember her still, so fondly. You should get in touch with her! Do you know where she is?"

"She is in the U.S. Studying Art. And there is no point contacting her. She already … has a boyfriend."

"Hmmm."

"So, you tell me, who all you have been in love with." He asks.

"Ok, first there was Sushant from sixth standard, then Vishal…"

And we talk and talk as the hours whiz past.

Rishika – Where do we go from here? This isn't where we intended to be. We had it all...

"I never thought that things could ever turn out to be the way they have." I sigh. "I mean… look at me… and look at you. A few months back we had these wonderful jobs that were paying so well. And now… we think forty times before we decide to go to a coffee shop and have a cup of decent coffee."

I fall silent

"Huh! And I was the one who used to think that we belong to a generation for whom earning money is not a big deal, and we seek higher satisfaction. I was so wrong. I was really living a deluded life." She looks down at the ground and says "Huh! And we are not even able handle the present financial condition. We are so not able to cope with this recession. We truly don't have control on ourselves."

We are sitting near the lake where Amit's birds come to spend the winters (that is how he always puts it). And he does not accept this, but I think he is losing hope of being able to save this piece of land. Which I think is the reason why he wanted to come here today before it gets dug up and destroyed.

"I don't think so Rishi." Amit says, "I mean I still believe that we are a part of the generation which seeks higher satisfaction. If I look at myself, I can think of no other reason than that for quitting my job and fighting to save this land. I agree I have no idea as to how and what I should do to save this land but… I would still fight. And we *are* earning. We *do* have jobs. Those may not be the best jobs on earth but we are still able to support ourselves. And if you did not have this crisis in your personal life, I am sure that you would also have followed a path that your heart directed you to."

I don't feel like saying anything. He may be right about whatever he is saying, but … somehow it does not make me want to say anything. These days I am constantly in a fix. I have lost all excitement. I have lost all interests. Life feels like an … aimless journey, which I have been forced to undertake.

"And if you talk about learning to handle our present financial condition, I would say that we may not have learnt to handle it, but we have definitely adjusted well.. I mean, I might still want to dine at the Taj, but I know that I can't afford it right now. It does not mean that I will never go and dine there, but I know that right now

I can't, and I will go when I have the money for it. And I think this adjustment in itself is quite an achievement. And this, I think, goes for both of us." Amit continues.

"May be you are right." I say looking around.

It is a beautiful landscape. There is a belt of trees that surround the lake that diminishes gradually as we move away from it. Its evening and the rays of the setting sun are bouncing off the surface of the water giving it a golden glitter. And I never knew there was so much wildlife just outside Gurgaon. I saw so many different kinds of birds I had never seen before. And we also a spotted deer. And that thing just vanished in a matter of seconds. Very shy creatures they are! I can almost understand why Amit feels so strongly about the environment. We humans have no right to destroy the habitat of other species.

"You know something, instead of town planning; you should have studied environmental sciences." I say.

"Huh. If only I knew myself that well when I was in the twelfth standard. Anyway. How is your book coming along?"

"I don't know yaar. I sent the first three chapters I wrote to a publisher and I did not get a positive feedback. They said that both the characters and the plot were very ordinary. And there was nothing special about the narration. So I don't really know how I am going to take it forward." I look at the ground, think for a moment and say,

"And you know what the worst part is? I don't *have* a story. I have no ending for my book.

Amit – He must do something about his environmental concerns.

It's a building in exposed brickwork. Complete Laurie Baker style. I check my notebook once again to confirm if I am at the right address. Yes, this is it. This is the office of the NGO 'Save the World'. And from what I have gathered, they have deep environmental concerns. It seems a nice and cozy place, a good ambience and full of plants I can hear a lot of birds chirping and there is also a lily pond, with lotuses in it. I approach the Reception counter and say,

"Hi, I am Amit. I have come here with a proposal to save a piece of land that is an environmental reserve but is soon going to be destroyed. It is home for a specific species of migratory birds that travel every year from Russia to that very piece of land in the winters." How much information am I supposed to give the receptionist? I really do not know. I pause. The receptionist is pretty with curly hair and big eyelashes and she is smiling as I speak.

I have not really figured out what to say when she says,

"I am sorry sir but we don't deal with environmental issues anymore."

"Oh. Is it?"

"Yes, sir. We work to help the poor dyslexic children now." She says beaming broadly at me.

Oh no! My birds are neither dyslexic nor … poor. Well, they may be poor but are certainly not dyslexic. Or even if they are, there is no chance of finding that out. How do I make them read? Vasay, what would they look like with glasses on?

"So if you want us to look into any case concerning dyslexia, we would be more than happy to help you."

People really get carried away with whatever Amir Khan does or say, don't they?

"No… I don't have any such case. Do you know any other …organization which deals with such environmental issues?"

"I am really sorry sir; I don't have any such information."

Rimy – She thinks taking one's clothes off is a sure short way to please people and go places.

Is Natasha obsessed with Kylie or what? I mean, if it was any other *great* artist I would understand. But *Kylie*? Natasha is dressed like the devil. And is dancing to the song '*I am better the devil you know*'. Yeah! You bet! Uh! And her dress also seems to act pretty deviously, lifting itself at strategic points. I will have to do better than that. Not that I mind a little skin show, but there is hardly anything left to show after all that Natasha has revealed. Not that I am feeling insecure or anything, but I know I am way better than her and she stands no chance in front of me. But Mannu Salik really likes her performance.

"Very tasteful. And with some very unique dance moves." He says.

Uh! Just wait till you see my moves. Anyway, let's see the next performance. Ah! I can't believe it!!! . The next contestant! She is wearing a blue chiffon saree and is dancing to '*Kate nahi katte yeh din yeh raat*'. What does she think of herself? Is she Sridevi? Uh! How disillusionalized can one get? Anyway, I gather all my patience and painfully watch the rest of this bunch. And finally Shekhar (along with Ravi) comes on stage. There is something about this guy. He sets foot on the stage and everything comes alive. . Beams of light start rotating around him as *he* moves to really cool pulsating music. I have not heard that music before but its' really catchy. He is doing everything, from somersaults to cartwheels to God knows what else. And Ravi is not that bad either, and is matching Shekhar step for step. It's like they have both set the stage on fire, literally, for towards the end of their performance they do a little fire-breathing stunt as well. Hmm.

Ok, its Kamal's turn next. He comes on stage with an acoustic guitar. Hmm, I wonder what he is going to do with that. He is singing another Hindi song again. Oh God! Is it going to be another Kishore Kumar number? Uh! I think I know this track. It is from the movie where Aamir Khan plays a child actor who finds it difficult to control his bladder. Actually now that I am listening to the song, I kind of like it. And the sound of the guitar also goes well with the song. It's that song yaar, '*Kya Hua Tera Wada, Voh Kasam, Voh Irada.*' Actually Kamal does play the guitar well, and he is not blindly singing the song but is also giving it some unique touches of his own. Hmm. Interesting. The judges also like it.

"Very interesting mix of Pop and Reggae you had there." Ranisha Sunoy says as she looks fondly at him. Hmm, he is becoming her favorite. I can *so* see that.

Oh! It's my turn next, and as I had decided, I performed '*Material Girl.*' I just love that song. I think it has the greatest beats ever. And as an answer to Natasha's skin revealing act, I have decided to shed some clothes on stage. My costume comprises a black mini skirt and a red jacket with a tiny short tube top under it. So what I have decided is that I am going to roll that tube top a little more, and take off my jacket while I perform. Will that be hot or what!?

And I do that, but unfortunately for me, just as I remove my jacket, the zipper gets stuck and there is a little awkward moment. But when I take it off, there is a lot of hooting. Everyone seems to like what I have just done. I shoot a look at Natasha, Huh! You think you can do better than this? I end my performance to a lot of clapping. I can hear some whistles too. . I look at all the other contestants and see Shekhar clapping like mad. So is Ravi. But Kamal is just sitting with his arms folded, and his face free of any expression. In fact, he is looking a little pissed off. And obviously Natasha has a super jealous expression. I turn around to look at the judges as I get the mic.

Mr. Naved Bukhtawar speaks first "It was a very bold performance Rimz." I love it when such great celebrities call me by my name. It's really cool.

"Yes sir." I say panting heavily, holding the mic with both my hands.

"But you know I just felt that most of the time you seemed to be eager to just take your clothes off."

Uh! I know it. He is so old fashioned that he can only disapprove!

"It was supposed to be a dance round, but you made it look more like a striptease round."

What nonsense, I am not the only one showing a little skin there, am I? Have they forgotten Natasha?

"But sir, there have been other contestants who also revealed quite a lot of themselves in the earlier performances." I say pointing to Natasha. And as I say this everyone falls silent; even the judges. After a moment that seems an eternity, Ranisha Sunoy speaks up,

"Rimz, if we are pointing you and only you out, there has to be a reason for it."

"Yes ma'am, and I just want to know that reason." Oh my God! I have offended the judges! I should apologize! What am I saying? What am I doing?

"We just think that what you did there was completely unnecessary," says Mr. Naved.

"Ok sir, I am sorry. I will plan my future performances more carefully." I say.

"You don't have to be sorry Rimz," Mannu Salik says, "I think it was a very bold performance and it really takes a lot of courage and confidence to do something like that and I think… it was good."

"I think you liked a lot of things apart from confidence Mannu," teases Ranisha.

Amit – Now which guy would like to go and shop with a girl for her wedding trousseau? But he still goes and does it.

"At times I really have my doubts about being able to save the bird land." I am talking to Rishika. It is a Saturday evening and Rishi and I are going out shopping for her wedding trousseau.

"Why? What happened now?" she asks her eyes fixed on the road ahead as she drives.

"I don't know; there is no positive sign that I see anywhere. It's complete… darkness everywhere."

"Hmm, hey. I have an idea. Why don't you contact some of the newspapers and explain the situation to them. If it gets written about then, I am sure it would become difficult to suppress."

"Hmm, yeah, good idea." I say.

"I will give you all the contacts I have. There is someone I know who might be able to help you."

"Cool."

We have reached the market and Rishi is looking for a place to park the car.

"You know how much I hate shopping right?" I say.

"Yes, I know. Too bad for you that Rimz is not here."

"I still can't believe that you are getting married." I say.

"I have stopped thinking about it." she says.

"Oh! How's your book coming along?"

"It's going on fine. I have finally figured out a research methodology. I am going to select fifty subjects and study their relationships and try to figure out the reason for the rising rate of divorces and break-ups these days. And out of those fifty subjects, two will be you and Rimz. And I am also going to float a questionnaire in all the states – 1000 questions in each, to draw a conclusion and then weave a story around it." she said as the car came to a halt.

"Hmm, sounds like a lot of work." I say as we get out of the car.

"Yeah."

"What are we here to shop for by the way?"

"My engagement ring." She says.

"Hmm. You have Iman's size right?"

"Why would I need his size for my engagement ring?" she says casually.

Wait a minute, I am confused. "You mean that you are going to buy a wedding ring for yourself?"

"Yes."

"That you would give it to Iman that day so that he could give it back to you?"

"Yes."

"It does not make any sense. And more over, isn't it bad luck?"

"It makes all the sense. And I don't believe in luck."

"But... where is the romance in it? Where is the mystery? What's the fun if you have already seen your engagement ring before it's offered to you?" I really can't believe my ears. It sure does kill all the fun and the excitement.

"I don't know about the others, but I would really feel awful wearing an ugly ring on my finger for life. I would rather not have any *mystery* but have an engagement ring of my choice."

"My God! You are weird. And is Iman doing the same?"

"Yes, he will buy the ring he likes himself."

"And he does not find it weird or... wrong."

"*No*! My God! What is *wrong* in it?"

"Nothing. You both are made for each other. Where are we going to have lunch by the way?"

"Uff! Can't you ever stop thinking about food? Anyway."

"Hmm."

"Hey! What happened to that spoilt brat from your school? Were you able to reach his father?"

"Not as yet. But I am supposed to meet him tomorrow. You didn't tell me where we gonna eat."

Rimz – a dinner under the stars.

Dinner is going to be served in a while. I sit here waiting. I am kind of worried after today's performance. Two out of the three judges do not like me. How am I going to win if this continues? It is *so* unfair! I mean Shekhar and Ravi also performed topless. No one said anything to them. I have a nice enough figure, so why can't *I* flaunt it? I am sure who ever watched me today, enjoyed the performance. Just then my phone starts to ring. It's Rishi,

"Hello." I say

"Rimz!!!! I just saw your show on TV! You so rock man!"

"Really?"

"Yes! You have become the Controversy Queen! I tell you girl; you are famous. There are articles in the newspapers about you. People have formed online communities in your name on Orkut and facebook. You are all over the place! This is so great. You are a star, girl!"

"Really? I am?"

"Yes! Anyway, I have to go now, Or else I will have to eat some burnt *bhindies*."

"Ok," I giggle.

"I'll call you later. And once again YOU ROCK!"

"Thanks." I smile

"Bye."

"Bye."

I sit there looking at the stars for a while. It's the first time I am feeling a little scared.

"It was quite a performance you pulled off there today."

It's Kamal. Great! It has been more than one and a half weeks and the only friend I have made is this *gawar*.

"Yeah," I say heavily, "My friend also just called, she says I am becoming really popular out there. And then she had to go… otherwise she would have had to eat burnt …*bhindies*."

"Uh! *Bhindies?* Reminds me of lizards. Talk about some burnt ones."

"Hey! Mc too. I meant *Bhindies* reminded me of lizards. I just can never eat them." I say.

He smiles. Yes, that is what he seems to be doing most of the time – smile. And then there is a short silence.

"It was a nice performance today. That was one of my favorite songs." I say.

"Thanks." He smiles again.

"Hey! You know what? I have not heard that song that you were telling me about the other day, the one you want to sing in the finals. Do you have it with you right now?"

"Yes I do, but please don't announce it like that. Someone might just steal the idea." He whispers.

"Ok." I whisper back as I let out a tiny, cute, giggle.

He takes out an mp3 player from his pocket and hands me the earphones. I plug them into my ears and the song starts.

I listen to the song carefully. It really is a nice one. It reminds me of each and every crush that I have ever had. I get so lost in the song that I don't even realize when it ends. Suddenly Kamal shakes me and I open my eyes, totally startled. "Rimz, RIMZ."

"Hmm? What?" I say

"The song is over."

"Yes."

"And they have served dinner also."

"Oh! Ok." I am still kind of lost

"Come."

"Yes." I get up like a zombie and follow him.

Amit – The things you do for kids.

It's Sunday and I can't believe how I am spending it! I am sitting here in front of this huge mansion in Ghitorni. Yes, I am in front of Rohit's house. And there is this huge gate, next to which stands this tall security guard. I have requested him to let me in to meet Rohit's father almost five times now but each time he has told me that Mr. Solanki is busy in a meeting and he is not sure when he will be available. But I am determined not to let him get away today. All week I have been leaving messages on the phone for him, mentioning that it is about his son, but there has been no response at all. And yes, I have also learned that the father is a very big shot, and active MP. And that is the reason he is so busy all the time in some meeting or the other. The parents are separated and that explains a completely neglected problem-child. I keep waiting and waiting and on failing to spot any activity finally tell the guard,

"You have got to let me in. You don't know how important it is."

He does not respond, does not even blink his eyes. It is like he can't see or hear me....and just then a car honks its horn from the inside. The guard leaps to open the gate and I see a white Ambassador with a red hooter thing on the top.

The father is leaving? Even when I have sent message after message that I have come from Rohit's school and want to speak with him urgently. Well, I am not going to let him get away this time round. I will make him speak with me. So as the car starts to move, I run alongside. "Mr. Solanki!" I frantically knock on the window adjacent to the important looking guy in the vehicle. The car keeps moving.

"Mr. Solanki wait! I need to talk to you!" Suddenly the car halts and some 4 black cat commandos leap out (I don't know from where) and grab hold of both my arms.

"Drop all your weapons." They say.

"What? I don't have any weapons! I am a... I am from Rohit's school. I need to talk to Mr. Solanki. It's about his son." how many times do I have to repeat that?

The important looking guy steps out of the car and walks towards me. He observes me for a few seconds and then asks.

"What is your name?"

"I am Amit, Amit Trehan. I am the counselor from your son's school. I need to talk to you about him." I say panting.

"Let him go." He orders his commandos.

The important looking guy fishes out his cell phone and calls someone.

"There is someone at the gate who wants to meet you." He says in the phone. The guy at the other end of the line says something and he disconnects the call.

"Let him in." he says.

Rima – Bhindis look like lizards.

"*Bhindi?*" I almost scream. I can't believe it. There is just one vegetable that we don't like and we just talked about it and that is what we are having for dinner.

"Yes, seems like God wants us to taste it today." Kamal smiles

"What? No! I have tried it so many times and I have never liked it! I am not having it! I will just have *daal* and *roti* today. And *raita* and salad, and ... this weird looking gravy dish."

"Oh come on Rima, be a sport. Let's try it. It will be fun." He says.

"No. No, no, no, no, *no!*"

"Yes. Yes, yes, *yes.*" He says putting a portion of *bhindi* on my plate as I gape at him in utter shock. We walk to our pet spot and sit down.

"Yuk! How can anyone eat this thing! It looks like fried lizards. And ... it is so ... slimy and greasy." I say as I put one in my mouth.

"Ha ha! I know, but you can't deny that you are having fun. It's written all over your face."

We are sitting face to face on the steps again with our plates in front of us. And yes, I can't really deny it; I am having fun.

"That is so not true. It's one of the worst times of my life."

"You are lying."

"Am not."

"Yes you are."

"No I am not."

Silence.

"Rimz can I ask you something?" he looks into my eyes and says.

"No."

"Why do you call yourself Rimz? Rima is so much better."

"Because it's more… trendy. It's more… it has spunk." I say. What is up with him?

"So it's all about showing off is it?" he says

"No it's not! It's about the essence. It's about the…"

"Rima why did you take off your jacket today?"

You know, actually, I am quite embarrassed about it myself.

But instead of admitting that, I say "Because I wanted to show that stupid Natasha that there is nothing that she can do and I can't."

"It should not be about showing her that you can also do what she can. It should be about showing her that there are things that *you* can do that *she* can't. That *you* are capable of doing something unique and original."

Silence.

Hmm, he does make a little sense.

"And if you really ask me, it should not be about showing anything to anyone. That is when things start to become superficial and unsubstantial. You should do it for yourself – for *your* own satisfaction – to bring you happiness. And if at all it is about anyone else, it should be about *convincing* them; telling them that you are good enough. Not showing them anything."

I have been staring at him all this while and I did not realize it till he started speaking again. "Rima, are you ok?"

"Yes, …yes. I am completely fine." I stammer.

"So you are a diehard Madonna fan?" he asks.

"Yes."

"Hmm, why do you like her so much?"

"Why do I like her so much? She is the best! Which other pop star do you know of who is fifty plus and still going as strong as '*Hard Candy*'? And also, she started a whole new culture. And all her songs, they talk about the strength of a woman. She is like *the best.* Anyway, you tell me, is there any actress or pop star that you like? Any *female* star that you find beautiful?" I ask.

"I think Audrey Hepburn was a really beautiful actress."

"Oh my God! Are you even …living in today's time? You are such an oldie!"

"Well, I don't think there is anyone as good as her today."

"Oh come on! Give me a break! Why won't you just admit that you don't have any idea about *who's who* in the glamour world today? Ah! You are so disillusionalized in life!"

Smiling, he looks at me and says, "you know that is no word, right?"

I gape at him wide-eyed with shock and offence, "Yes it is!" and what does he know about the English language? He is such a *gawar*!

Very confidently he replies, "No its not. And about the actresses of today – I just feel that their problem is that they are very scared and insecure. That is why that they give in to all the pressure and go out half-clad just to show some sex appeal, which is perhaps easier for them to possess. I mean, have you ever gone through those 'entertainment' magazines?"

I can sense anger in his speech as he goes on.

"No one is bold enough to go ahead with a nice, cute, feel-good look like we used to have before. No! They feel the pout will work all the time and…" he trails off into silence. But I am still thinking about what he has just said.

"I am sorry… I think I just got a little carried away," he says, "How does it matter who does what these days?"

"Hmm, yeah."

"I was just thinking, maybe for the next round – the duets round, how about performing together?" Kamal says.

"Hmm, it's not a bad idea. But what would we sing?"

"There are so many songs. We would surely be able to pick up something nice."

"But please don't make me sing any of your stupid Hindi songs. I just won't be able to do that." I say

"Ok, we could sing '*Lucky*' that Jason and Colbie duet."

"YES! We can do that! I love that song!!!!! . *Vasay* what did you have in mind when you asked me to perform with you for the last round?" I ask him.

"I was planning to play 'Classical Gas' on my guitar as you could have danced to it," he says

"Yeah; that would have been cool." I have no idea what 'Classical Gas is! And I have always been terrible at Chemistry *and* History.

"Cool then. Hey! Look, your Shekhar is here." He says as he sees him going towards the buffet table.

"Hmm, what? I mean why did you say My Shekhar … I mean

your Shekhar? He is not mine. I mean… why would you say that?"

"Rima, who are you fooling here. Everyone knows that you have the biggest crush on him. And I must tell you that you are not alone. There are four other girls in line."

"Yeah, I know that," I say as I start to think of what I can do about it.

"You know, I think he has a girlfriend. Would it be a good idea to become friends with Ravi and get to know more about Shekhar?"

"No Rima, he does not have *a* girlfriend. He has *a number* of girlfriends. But you can still try if you want to."

"Uh! You are just jealous."

"No I am not." he denies.

"Yes you are." I repeat.

"No I am not."

"Oh just shut up! He is coming here."

I sit in anticipation and Kamal sits quietly next to me as Shekhar approaches us.

"Hi,' he says.

"Hi," I say with a pleasant, smile.

"Quite a performance you delivered today."

"Thanks."

"I was wondering, maybe we could get together in the next round for the duets?" he asks.

Is this true? Is he really asking me to join him?

"Hey! That would be so cool. Thanks."

Thanks? Why the hell am I saying thanks when I could have just said "Yeah, sure," as casually as possible?

"Cool then. See you tomorrow morning at the rehearsals hall."
He says

"Cool. See you tomorrow!" I say to his departing back.

I turn around and look at Kamal all excited. He is smiling at me. Oh damn! I just promised him…

My expression suddenly changes and I blurt, "Sorry."

"It's ok, I understand."

Amit – How rich could people get in life?

Is it a house or a palace? I really can't say. Everything is endless about this place. The ceilings are so high – endless; the rooms are so big – endless; the sofas are so long – endless! And the kind of appliances and fixtures used in the house… God! It's crazy! The room where I sit has this water feature on one wall, which ends in a pool at the floor. And the pool is glittering golden. I get up and go closer to the water feature to get a better look. The bottom of the pool is lined with golden tiles. Somehow it gives me the impression of being very expensive.

"It's laminated gold foil." I hear a voice say from behind.

I turn around startled and nearly trip into the water, as I turn to see a young looking man standing there. He must have been in his early thirties.

"It's good *feng shui*. We are still to put fish in it." he says as he comes and sits on the majestic sofa.

"You really impressed my Dad." He says.

"Oh! That was your father! I am really sorry about the scene. I didn't know…" I stammer.

"It's ok. Come sit."

And very obediently I seat myself.

"Now tell me. What brings you here?"

"It's about your son, Sir. He is not at his best behavior in school." I pause before proceeding. I do not want to shock him "Mr. Solanki he is stealing things from other children." I say in a serious, grave tone.

Silence.

"And that is not all. He also gets violent and … fights with other children."

"Are you sure about what you are saying Mr. Amit?"

"Yes Sir I am very sure. The other day he stole a pencil from this sweet little girl and when she said that she had seen him taking the pencil, he hit her with a pencil box."

"This is outrageous."

"It sure is Mr. Solanki. And I would want you to pay attention to the matter." I can see anger flaring in his eyes.

"But you must deal with the matter with utmost care. I mean … beating the kid won't be of any use." I stammer.

"It's shocking. I have never deprived my son of anything."

All of a sudden it all becomes clear to me. It's a typical case of neglecting one's child – the father is incredibily rich. He thought that by giving his son everything he could possibly afford, the child could be kept happy. But in actuality, the method has failed miserably. All the kid wants is his father's attention and love.

"Just try talking to him at times. Don't mention that you got these complaints about him. Just talk to him… like a father would talk to his son."

He keeps looking at me and says, "I want you to keep reporting to me."

Rimz – She is going on a date with Shekhar (!!!!!)

It's 8:15 PM and I am almost ready. Just need to put on the earrings. Shekhar is supposed to come at 8:30 and I don't want to keep him waiting. Natasha has somehow figured out that I am going out with Shekhar tonight and I don't want to take any chances. If I make him wait, who knows what she might do? For all I know, she could make him change his mind or worse…go on a date with him, leaving me behind. Ok, I am all ready. Just … 13 minutes to go and he will be here.

All right, I am still waiting. 20 minutes have past and now there is still no sign of Shekhar. I have already gone into the hall and peeped outside the window thrice. Last time Natasha caught me peeping. She is talking to someone on the phone and overhear her saying, "Rimz is hovering around in the cottage like a humming bird. She is so excited about going out with Shekhar."

Huh! How jealous can one get?

Anyway, I nervously look at my watch. It is 8:45. I really don't want to be stood up. Hmm. Ok, there is one way to get this right. If Shekhar does not turn up, I will go out with Kamal and tell everyone that I cancelled the date with Shekhar because plans had already been made with Kamal. Yes, that sounds good. I will do that. Just then I hear the horn outside. I run to the door, stand there for a second. Catch up my breath, and I open the door with a smile.

"*There* you are!" I say beaming. He is on a red bike and is looking awesome. He is wearing a white T-shirt with a pair of blue jeans. It is dark outside, and he is still wearing shades. Ummm, that look is totally from the 80's but who cares? He looks great!

"Cool bike." I say as I walk around and sit on it.

"Thanks," he flashes a smile.

"Ready?" he asks as I settle down.

"Ready." I say

And away we go.

Amit – Heal the world, make it a better place.

I have come to this coffee shop thousands of times. But I think it's for the first time that I have come here for something serious – something worth doing. I am meeting the journalist here today (the one Rishi was talking about the other day.) and while I wait for her, I think I should … have a nice, warm cup of Darjeeling tea. Yes, that is what I should do; I should order a cup of tea. I catch the waiter's eye and place my order.

Its been here for about fifteen minutes I have been waiting and I have noticed every single person walking through that door. And there has been no sign of anyone who looks anything like a journalist. Yes, there has been no one who has come in wearing a *khadi kurta* with a *jhola* slung on her shoulder. Everyone looks hip and modern, like the girl who has just entered. She is tall, with long, curly hair and a fair, round face, slightly long top worn over jeans. I am sure she is a TV star. They are all over the place these days. The other day when we were having dinner at a restaurant, (back when we used to have jobs) we spotted one. And no one even got up to get an autograph from her. Poor thing I wonder how a 'star' would feel if no one around them asked for autographs. Anyway, how do I care? I turn my gaze back to my table and focus on the cup of tea.

"Excuse me." Ok, there is someone hovering around who wants to talk to me.

"Yes." I say as I look up.

"Is your name Amit, by any chance?" It is the girl who just entered the coffee shop, the one who I was imagining to be a TV star. But why would such a girl look for me? Has the underworld got involved in this birdland business? Am I in danger?

"Yes. Why? Is that some thing bad? I mean… should I not be … Amit?"

"Not at all." she says as she laughs, "I am Jyoti, from Bharati Times." She says as she hands me a business card.

"Oh! You are the *journalist*." Wow! I mean … WOW!!

She smiles back at me. There is an awkward moment of silence and then I realize I should be polite!

"Please, sit." I offer.

"Thank you," she says as she sits down.

"So," she starts, "about the conservation project."

"Yes, that is very important. The land of the foreign birds." I say with utter zest.

She gives me a weird look and then, says, "Yes. Tell me about it."

"Ok, see, there is a lake about twenty kilometer south of Gurgaon. And each year…" wait she does not look that interested. I have to explain everything differently in order to gain her interest.

"Wait, let me start with how the whole of 'new' Gurgaon was developed." I say.

"Ok."

"Long back, all this land was nothing but a cluster of villages. And the villagers were mainly into farming and looking after their cattle. The natural vegetation was … essentially a mix of trees that could survive harsh climate, and so were not very high in number. There were also many thorny shrubs and bushes given this belt only descends down to Rajasthan and turns into the Thar Desert. The region that we now see as the cosmopolitan town full of tall glass buildings, all high tech and everything, was therefore actually only pieces of land mostly owned by the villagers. Some pieces were inhabited by humans and the whole of this region had an ecological balance back then. Each occupied or 'unoccupied' land had its own function and importance. As the National Capital of New Delhi started overflowing with… everything, people identified these pieces of lands as regions with great potential. And soon it caught the attention of the 'big' builders who started buying these pieces of land from the villagers, and started planning towns and colonies there. Different builders bought land from different owners. And that is actually the reason why all the 'towns' and 'colonies' have such jagged and confusing boundaries."

She was listening to all this and nodding. Great! It was working!!

"This rampage of buying and 'developing' went on." I continued. "The rich builders kept on making money. The wild deer and buffaloes went on losing their habitat. And now this lake and the area around it are in danger. This region plays host to special migratory birds that come all the way from Russia, in the winters. And you know how important it is for the ecology to have them continuing to come here. I mean so many plant species depend on that!"

"It's really nice to know that how strongly you feel about the environment." She says My eyes are almost popping out as I take a pause to catch my breath. I was speaking with such vigour and so...fast. "If all of us start feeling the way you feel, it would bring a huge change,"

"I *know!*" I say.

"And good to know that you know so much about the region. Most of the youth just comes here to rave about the buildings and malls." She says. I like this girl. She is sensitive (towards the environment)

"Ya, thanks. I know all this because I am a town planner and have been working with these builders for a while now. And you know, all this is nothing compared to the garbage management story."

"Garbage management story?" she asks.

"Yes, the garbage management story. The infrastructure of this place is terrible. Keep aside the road networks and the electricity. Not even the sewerage systems are in place."

"Hmm, interesting." She says.

"Yes. All these multistoried housing colonies and the shiny office buildings – most of them do not have the necessary sewerage connections. Most of them have underground tanks, which collect all the waste, which is later dumped in to these huge trucks and taken away.

"Really?" she looks shocked now.

"*Yes.*" Oh God! She does not know. I must tell her! "And you would be even more shocked to know where they dump all the garbage – the toilet waste – *the night soil.*"

"Where do they dump it?" she asks.

"At the foothills of the Arravalis!" I say.

"Oh no!"

"Oh yes. And you should try going there sometime. It is so terrible! All the animals and birds have fled the place. Only flies and mosquitoes thrive there."

"That is such a threat to the health of the people."

"I know! And you know what? The other day I went there, and I saw a *dead camel.*" I say as I trail into silence.

"That is terrible." She says.

"And that is not all, you would be shocked further to know the actual figures of the treated and the untreated sewerage that is disposed off."

Silence.

"According to the authorities, 60% of the waste is disposed off after it is treated, and 40% without being treated."

"40%! That is a huge figure." She says.

"Hah! But that is just a cover up. The actual figures are even more outrageous."

She looks at me with shocked, questioning eyes.

"10% treated, and 90% untreated."

Silence and shock.

Rimz – she could have never imagined that Shekhar was ...

Ok, the restaurant we go to, is not the best…it isn't the most romantic place but how does it matter? I like pizza anyway. We are at Pizza Hut and are eating pasta, and exotic garlic bread.

The waiter comes and takes our order "One veg pasta in mushroom sauce, and one in tomato sauce, and a pitcher of iced tea."

"Would you like it with spaghetti or Fuseli?"

I really find the word - 'fusli' funny and can never pronounce it correctly. !

"I would like to have it with spaghetti, what would you like it with?" Shekhar asks me.

Oh no!

"I would like to have it with fushli." I just fumble on the last word so that the waiter can just about hear the 'f' part of the word, and understand.

"You mean Fuseli, ma'am?" the waiter asks.

"Yes, can't you hear properly? What's wrong with his ears?" I look at Shekhar passing a what-is-wrong-with-him gesture as I let out a little laugh as the waiter leaves.

"So, how do you like it here?" Shekhar asks me.

"Oh! I love it, the thrill, and the idea that we are being observed all the time… … everything! The performances, the excitement… it's all so wonderful."

There is silence as he keeps looking at me for a while. Oh my God he looks so much like Robert Redford! I smile at him naughtily and ask, "Do you know who you look like?"

"No! And this is the second time you are asking me that? Please tell me!" he says

"You should find out for yourself." I tease.

"Oh come on!" he says throwing up his hands.

I smile mysteriously, "So, tell me, which was that movie that completely changed your life?" I ask him

He laughs and does not say anything.

"Oh come on! There is always a movie that changes your life! Which one was yours?"

"None comes to mind right now. You tell me, which one was yours?"

"No, not fair, if you won't tell me, then I can't tell you." How can I share my most intimate secret with him when he is not being honest with me? Everyone has that movie! I can't have a heart to heart chat with him if he is not ready for that.

"Ok, tell me, why have you come here? I mean, to this contest?" I ask him.

"Hmm, because I need to gain publicity before my film releases."

I almost choke on my drink. What? Is he an actor? He is a *hero!*

"Wow! Are you an actor?" I ask.

"Yes." He says with a smile. Oh my God! He is smiling at the table. Shy...I like shy guys. "Have you acted in anything else before... or this is your first mopie? I mean movie." God! What is wrong with me?

"It's my first mopie." He says with a smile. Oh how cutely he imitates me!

"How did you make it to the movie? I mean how did you... get the role?" I have to figure this out and follow the same route. He smiles mysteriously and after a pause, says, "My father is a film producer."

!!!!!!!!!!!!!!!!!!

Amit – His life is so gonna change now.

The alarm goes off again in the morning. It is funny isn't it? Every morning I set the alarm for 5:30 AM. And every morning I keep putting it on the snooze mode for a full hour. So I finally only get out of bed by 6:30! This is nothing new; it has been on since I was in the eighth standard. It's really true what they say – old habits die hard! I get out of the bed sluggishly and drag myself to the main door. "What do we have in today's newspapers?" I mutter.

Hmm, *Eight people die in a blast in Assam, Angry mob blocks traffic and burn tires in Gurgaon* (again), *Gurgaon's natural environment facing a threat.* Hmm… What? Wait a minute. That is the story I had told the journalist about. I sit down at the dining table and read the whole article very carefully. YES!!! IT IS THE STORY!!! THEY HAVE MENTIONED EVERYTHING!!! *IT'S IN THE NEWSPAPERS*!!! OH MY GOD! I CANT BELIEVE IT! I am so excited that I want to call Rishika and, thank her! I rush to my room to get my phone. But then I remember. Rohit, has stolen my phone. THAT STUPID KID-THIEF STOLE MY PHONE! Ok, note to self:

– *Must buy a new phone (by all means).*

Amit – He does not get to but a new phone after all.

Newsflash – I have got my phone back. If you really ask me, it is kind of disappointing, as I have been visiting the Nokia and Ericsson websites and poring over their funky new models while short listing a few. They really have some amazing phones in their series. Really cool ones. Anyway, what use is it now? I have got my stupid phone back. I am now well and truly stuck with it. Do you know how I got my phone back? Well, it happened just the way I lost it. I went inside the classroom – IIIrd B, and there it was, lying on the table. I didn't ask anyone or say anything. I just smiled at Rohit who avoided all eye contact.

Now it turns out that the children are really growing fond of me. I can see happiness in their eyes when they see me. They even get me flowers and handmade cards. They draw pictures of us playing together with flowers and butterflies and rainbows and everything. It's really sweet.

It's lunchtime and I am wondering what they are going to send up for lunch.

"May I come in Sir?"

Oh! It's Shikha. The child comes everyday to report Rohit's behavior.

"Hey! Shikha! Come come!"

She smiles and comes in "So, how's it going?"

"It's good sir."

"Great! So, what's the update?"

"He has not stolen anything sir."

"Great! And any fights?"

"No sir, no fights also."

"Wonderful!" It is the sixth day in a row. No complaints about Rohit! "So, what else? How's Benz now?" Benz is Shikha's dog and he has not been well; he ate some ... small animal and had been puking ever since.

"He is a lot better now sir."

"Great! Is he eating properly now?"

"Yes sir."

"Cool. So what have you got for lunch today?"

I kind of like my new job!

Rimz – She never knew she could feel like this.

> *Never knew I could feel like this*
> *Like I've never seen the sky before*
> *I want to vanish inside your kiss*
> *Every day i'm loving you more than this*
> *Listen to my heart, can you hear it sings*
> *Telling me to give you everything*
> *Seasons may change, winter to spring*
> *But I love you until the end of time*
> *Come what may*

I can't believe it is actually happening!!!!! . I am singing with Shekhar on stage!!! . With Shekhar!!! . The son of a film producer!!!! . Oh my

God, it's my turn and I have to sing .I look at him shyly and start.

Suddenly the world seems such a perfect place
Suddenly it moves with such a perfect grace
Suddenly my life doesn't seem such a waste
It all revolves around you

The applause is deafening I don't realize it but I am so excited that I am breathing heavily. Everyone is clapping hard and I can't stop smiling. Shekhar is also very happy. He puts an arm around my waist and gives me a hug.

Oh my God! Now I am blushing. The judges are going to give their verdict now.

"Mind blowing, it was a mind blowing performance. Both of you were too good. And Rimz, you were simply excellent! All the notes correctly sung... everything just perfect!" that is Mannu Salik.

"I agree with Mannu today. It was a very good performance." Says Ranisha Sunoy

Naved Bukhtawar is looking at us silently. He still hates me so he won't say anything good.

"Rimz, you surprised me today." he says. And there is a loud round of applause.

"Last time I told you that you lacked expressions, but today ...Are you both actually going around?" he asks with a frown.

I blush and mumble, "No sir," into the mic.

"Then why are you blushing?"

Am I still blushing? I can feel my cheeks growing warm!

"I am just pulling your leg. But excellent performance, both of you."

"Thank you sir." We both say.

Ok, it is Kamal's turn next. He is singing with Natasha. Hmm, I am not surprised. He had told me that he could not find anyone else to sing with him, but I think he has fallen for her. She has such long legs. Huh! But how do I care? The drum beats begin and Kamal starts singing.

Do you hear me?
I'm talking to you
Across the water across the deep blue ocean
Under the open sky, oh my, baby I'm trying

And then Natasha starts,

Boy I hear you in my dreams
I feel whisper across the sea
I keep you with me in my heart
You make it easier when life gets hard
And then they both sing together,
I'm lucky I'm in love with my best friend
Lucky to have been where I have been
Lucky to be coming home again
Ooohh oooohh oooh oooh ooh ooh ooh ooh

Uh! Ooh ooh ooh! Just look at her holding his hand like that! What a !@@$@^^*()

They don't know how long it takes
Waiting for a love like this

They sing the whole stupid song. Anyway, I am keen to hear what the judges have to say.

Ranisha – "Kamal. You are my favorite. And once again you have made me proud of you."

What *is* it with her?

Mannu – "Well done Natasha. Wonderful performance. And great chemistry you both had there."

Naved – "I am really amazed. I mean … such great talent we have out here. I don't think it's fair to have this competition – everyone is *so* good!"

Yes, yes.

"Thank you so much sir, thank you so much." They both say as they leave the stage smiling.

Rishika – Who lives happily after getting married?

"It's not working. It's just not working. Everything is falling apart." I say shaking my head.

"Rishi, it's the third time you have said that without actually telling me what is *actually* not working. *Please*, chill; relax. Everything is going to be fine." Amit says trying to console me as I drive him home.

"How can you say that, you don't even know what is wrong!" I am almost on the verge of hyperventilating.

"Well, how will I know if you won't tell me?" He says.

"Huh!"

Silence.

"Ok. Are you going to tell me what is wrong?" he asks again.

"Are you deaf? Can't you hear? I said *everything*!" I am really frustrated now.

"Ok, so let's take it one by one. What's wrong with you and Iman now?" he asks.

"Everything."

He stares at me. I look at him from the corner of my eye.

"I don't think I like him anymore." I say flatly.

"And why is that?"

"Because I don't like him."

"Yes, I got that. But why is that so?" he asks.

"One, because he is a different person altogether. And two, I think he is cheating on me."

"What? Why would you think that? God! You really have *some* imagination, don't you?"

"Because he talks differently. He is … not interested in talking anymore. When I call him in the evening all he wants to do is sleep."

"Ok, does it occur to you that he could be tired?"

"He is not tired. I know him. He is cheating on me."

"You know something? Girls really amaze me at times. You all are supposed to be more sensitive and … mature. Then, how can you not understand things like these? But anyway, that is besides the point. So you completely doubt him?"

Ok, now he is really getting on my nerves. Instead of understanding my situation, and comprehending my plight, instead of any kind of … empathy, … he is taking Iman's side!

"I do not doubt him. I am sure." I say flatly.

"Yes, I meant that only."

"Yes."

"But you would still need to prove it. Why don't you hire a private detective to find it out?" he says.

Ok, maybe he has a point. I have no proof. Perhaps my problems and current situation is making me blind and I am not being able to see things clearly. And I should hire a detective only then will I have an unbiased opinion and a correct observation of the whole thing.

"Yes, I should do that."

"What? Wait! I was … joking."

He looks at me and realizes that I was not kidding. "Oh come on! You can't be serious!"

"Yes I am. And he would get me some photographs also. Just like they show in the movies."

"You are joking right? Please tell me you are joking. I don't want to believe that my best friend has become a lunatic."

"No I have not. Anyway. That is one thing. The other is the stupid job I took up. It's just …"

"But that is temporary. It's just for the time being, so you don't need to worry about it. Next." he says.

"And the stupid book I am writing. The whole methodology has completely fallen flat."

"Why? What happened?"

"It's not working. I floated the questionnaire and instead of an expected 26,000 replies, I got just 120."

"Hmm."

"But I think its ok. I am going to do what everyone else does. I am going to write a story based on our lives." I say.

"Yeah you could do that. There's no harm in that." he says casually. "I really don't mind the publicity. I mean, you should base at least one character on me."

"Yes." I say.

"By the way, that's my house. So we need to … stop." He says.

"Oh!" I push the brakes hard. God! What is the matter with me? I have never been so absent minded!

I open the door and step out. "Why don't you come up? We can order food and stuff." He says

"No yaar. I need to go. I need to go and … write!"

Rimy – as we said earlier, she never knew she could feel like this. And now she is going to fight with Kamal.

"Why did you choose her Kamal? Out of all the available girls around, why did you pick her?" I demand. Such a jerk! HE PICKS UP THAT SLUTTY NATASHA!!!!

"Hey! Relax! It's not that I am going around with her or something! We just sang a song together. And I didn't ask her to sing with me, she did. And who can say no to Natasha?" And why is she so important any way? who *is* Natasha?

"I don't know... not my friend…an enemy….maybe?" I shoot back.

"Oh please, why do you consider her an enemy?" he asks.

"Because she is evil! And I hate her! You could have sung with anyone else but her. But *no*, you had to sing with her only! Uh! You are … pathetic!"

"I am pathetic? *I* am pathetic? Oh God! You are going to be a difficult wife someday." he says.

"What? *What?* Who the hell do you think you are? I don't like you." I say pointing at his nose. "You are the worst person I have ever come across. Don't ever talk to me again. You were, you are, and you always would be A GAWAR! Yes! That's what you are, a *gawar*!" I get up and look at the buffet table.

"Dinner is served. And don't follow me. I am not going to have dinner with you ever again." I lash. He looks at me stunned. He looks kind of shocked. Hurt, actually. Well, that serves him right. All guys are bastards…All of them!

I go to the buffet table and serve myself. Then I hear a voice say "What happened Rimz? Alone today?"

I turn around to see Shekhar.

"Oh hi! No, no special reason. Just like that." I say.

"Come, let's sit." He says. And we dine together.

See, people like me, even the guy who I am in love with. I won't be left all alone if I don't talk to that stupid Kamal! Shekhar and I, we have just had dinner together and he has asked me to go out with him again this coming Saturday – after the next performance. I get up, put the plates in the bin, and say 'Good night, see you" before we part.

When I turn around to see the spot where Kamal and I would have dinner, I see him sitting all alone. His plate looks untouched and his head is turned the other way. He looks pathetic. Good for him. I should just leave him like that. Or maybe I should go and bid him goodbye. Like for the last time.

I walk over to him.

"Hi." I say.

"Hi." He says.

"Why didn't you eat your dinner?" I ask.

"Because I didn't feel like. And why would you care?"

He looks really sad and upset. He is not even looking at me while talking.

"Come on now, have dinner. It's not good... not to have dinner. Here, now eat." I pick up his plate and try giving it to him. He turns his face away, "I don't want to," he says. And I can see tears in his eyes. Oh my God what have I done? Have I hurt him? I am his only friend and he does not even feel like having food if I am not around. What have I done? I am such a ... bitch! Oh no!

"I am sorry." I say. "I should not have behaved the way I did."

"You don't have to. I am used to it," he says.

"Used to what?"

"Used to being treated the way you did. Its' not the first time a friend has behaved like that and left."

"Really? But why? You are such a nice person!" I say surprised.

Silence.

"Look Kamal. I am sorry. I should not have behaved that way and said the things I said. Now stop being this foolishness and have your dinner." I force the plate into his hands. "I have said sorry like a thousand times. And I never say sorry to anyone." I say

"I am sorry too." He says softly. "I should have thought more before saying 'yes' to Natasha. And you did not say sorry a thousand times. You just said that twice."

"Oh my God! You were counting?"

"Well I am not deaf you know." he says while beginning to eat. I lean back against the step. It's a beautiful night.

"So many stars. Isn't that beautiful?" I say gazing at the stars.

Silence. And after a while Kamal says, "You know what I find most amazing about them? The fact that when we look at them, we are looking back in time."

"Hmmm" I don't really understand and neither am I in the mood to ask. I just want to keep looking at the sky.

"Kamal, which was the movie that made all the difference in your life?" I ask him. "I am sorry but the stars have made me philosophical."

He smiles and keeps looking at the sky, "I will tell you, but you tell me first."

"No you go first."

"No, you!"

"No! I asked first, so you answer!"

"Ok, fine. Hmm, well for me there is no movie that *changed my life* as such, but yes, a movie made me think differently. It was *Finding Neverland*." He says

"What? *Finding Neverland*? What is so special about that?"

"Well, it taught me that inspiration can come from the smallest of things – the ones you may never even realize, unless you open your eyes."

Hmm, he does think deep doesn't he?

"Your turn." He says looking at me.

"Well for me it was *Chaalbaaz.*"

"Hmm, and why?"

"Well… I don't know, I just saw that movie and I felt so strongly that this is what I want to become! I just saw Sridevi as a dancer and that was it for me. After watching that movie I just knew what I wanted to be in my life. The song *kissi ke haath na ayegi yeh ladki* just *defined* me. It felt as if I was singing that out to the whole world!"

Silence. All I see is a smile on Kamal's face

"Ok, now tell me which was your most embarrassing moment?" I ask.

"What? Is this an interview round or something? And … I don't remember that." he stammers.

"Shut up. It's clear from your face that you have a very distinct embarrassing moment in your mind right now."

"Ok, it's not that big a deal, it's not that embarrassing anyway. It just used to be a little embarrassing when I was a kid. Back in school children used to call me Kamla."

"Oh my God!" I am in splits. His friends used to call him Kamla. *Aye Kamla rani, kidhar ja rahi ho? Aye Kamla rani yeh tum kya gaa rahi ho?* Oh my God!

"It's not that funny ok!" he says.

"Yes, yes, I am sorry." Oh my God! I have tears in my eyes from laughing so hard!

"Ok, your turn now."

"Ok, back in school children used to call me Rimz Saxena, sexy sena. And I really used to get bugged. Actually I kind of used to like it. But I used to pretend that I didn't like it."

Actually that is not my most embarrassing moment. My most embarrassing moment was when one of my colleagues stole my personal diary and read it out loud in the office that *Jhoom Barabar Jhoom* and *Tashan* were two of my favorite movies, and that I was a serious *Tashanaitus* patient and took sick leave to see the first day first show of the movie. For an entire month after that, I was laughed at for having bizarre and horrible tastes.

"So that's not your most embarrassing moment." He protests.

"Ammm, yeah, that maybe true. But we are not friends enough that I tell you my most embarrassing moment."

"Hey! That's cheating."

"Yes, that's what I am. A cheater."

"Not fair."

"Well, life itself isn't fair!"

Actually that's not my line. I have heard that in one of the movies.

"Anyway, now that we are officially friends, we should exchange our phone numbers." I say taking my cell phone out. "Tell me what your phone number is, I'll give you a missed call."

"I don't have a cell phone," he says matter-of-factly

"WHAT? What era are you from?" Good God! It's almost like he has gone back in time gazing at the stars. (May be that is what he meant!)

"I think that cell phones are a complete nuisance. They kill discipline. That little thing keeps ringing all the time. No matter where you are – in the middle of a meeting… everywhere!"

"But what if you have to make an emergency phone call? What if you are stuck somewhere and are getting really bored and need to call someone to talk?" I ask, shocked.

"Well if I get bored, I can handle it, I have other stuff like my music player. And about the emergency calls – I don't go to jungles. And these days you have S.T.Ds and P.C.Os everywhere."

My God! You are such a weirdo!

Silence.

"Tell me one thing Rima. You saw Sridevi playing that role in a movie and that is why you want to become a pop star?" he asks seriously.

"Yeah… but …why do you ask?" I ask him.

"Nothing really. A great man once said, why most people fail to perform well in their professions is that they are there for the wrong reasons. The desire for fame and recognition; the urge to make big money, are not the right reasons to choose what one should do."

Hmm. Hmmmm. Oh what the hell! Why am I listening to someone who lives in another time period altogether!

Amit – He gets a letter from someone. (Oh no! is it the underworld threatening him to stay away from the birdland business?)

It's working! It's actually working! It's the third consecutive day that the newspapers have featured an article on the subject. I read the article sipping my tea at work. It feels great being a part of such a good cause. This is great! I see peon in the doorway, then.

"Hey! Ramesh! Come in." I say.

"Good morning sir."

"Good morning Ramesh."

"There is a letter for you sir."

"For me? That is weird. Who in this world would send me a letter?" I say

Oh no! Wait a minute! It's the mafia. The construction Mafia. They have figured out that I am the cause of the ... revolution and the series of articles and they have decided to ... threaten me. Or worse, KILL ME!! Oh no! My ex boss and that Shobha have thrown their lot in with the mafia! OH NO!!!!! Trembling like a leaf, I take the envelope.

"Thanks Ramesh." I manage a smile.

He nods and leaves. It is so strange... how life can just take a sudden turn without warning. How am I ever going to get out of this? I don't even know anyone on the police force. I struggle to open the envelope. It's a white piece of paper, with some writing in blue ink. I start reading.

Dear Amit,

This is to...

Wait a minute! Does the mafia address their victims as 'dear? Uh! Need to think about that later. Let's read the letter first!

Dear Amit,

This is to express my gratitude for the help you offered my son to overcome the bad habits he had developed. I am getting reports (not only from you, but from all the people who help in the house) that there is a marked difference in Rohit's behavior. These days I make it a point to spend time with him. Every evening I sit with him and we discuss everything from school to his friends. I must also add that he is growing really fond of you. Everyday our conversation starts with him telling me, 'Today Amit sir told us...' And from what I gather I think you have a marvelous way of explaining things to children. Rohit is a huge fan of yours. And when I told him that I was going to tell you this, he almost freaked out and requested me not to, to avoid embarrassment. .

Thank you for everything you have done.

I am hosting a dinner party this weekend at my farmhouse. I would be really delighted if you could come.

Warm regards

Amar Solanki

See, there is no need to freak out. It is fine. A powerful politician is inviting me to a party. Now even if the mafia threatens me, *I have links*!

Amit – Some things are moving,
Some things have got stuck.

"So Mr. Hot Shot, attending all the parties and everything?" Rishi teases me.

"Oh come on, you know it's not a big deal."

"Not a big deal! Oh please! You have initiated a series of articles that are getting recognized internationally, and, famous politicians are throwing parties as a gesture of gratitude for you."

Oh, I forgot to mention this but the series of articles have been recognized by *World Environment Organization* - (WEO), and the topic is becoming huge for environmentalist in various parts of the world. There has been a special rally in Paris as per news reports and people are marching on the roads, dressed up in costumes that look like birds and are holding placards saying 'Save us! Save us!' and the host for the show has also said that rumor has it that Pussycat dolls are all set to release a single that would convey the message of saving migratory birds of the world. And as I watched all this on the television the other day, I kept dreaming that one day they would feature an interview on '*the guy who started it all*'.

"Hmm, anyway. You tell me, how's your book coming along?" I ask.

"Oh please don't ask. It's terrible!"

"What? Why?"

"I really don't know what my heroine should do with her life. Her wedding is like in a week's time and she is having second thoughts about the guy she is going to marry. Should she end the doubts and stick to the commitment, or she should rethink it through?"

"I think she should stick to the commitment." I say taking a sip of my coffee.

Rimz – People are so jealous of her. Or are they?

I get up a little early today and am ready twenty minutes before breakfast is served. I am in the cottage and waiting in the living room, browsing the newspaper when Natasha comes out of her room wearing a short dress (as always), and her hair dripping wet.

"Hmm, this is something I never thought I would ever get to see

– Rimz reading a newspaper." she says.

Oh God! She has just woken up and got ready, and these are the first words she utters, although irritated, I am not going to react today.

"So tell me Rimz, is there a secret section in the paper from where you learn all your provocative and vulgar dance moves?"

Oh my God! She is such a bitch.

"Huh! You are just saying that because you know that I am better than you, and you are jealous that Shekhar is going out with me and not you."

She laughs throwing her head back. "Oh come on." she says, "you really think that I would be jealous of you because of that? And now that you have mentioned this new '*romance*', I think you must know a little more about it."

"What do you mean?"

"Shekhar is not going around with you because he is in *love* with you."

"Hah! What do you know?"

"Everything darling. He is going around with you because he made a bet with Ravi that he would kiss you within two weeks of knowing you."

"Oh my God! Just look at you! How jealous could one get in life? We both know why you are saying what you are saying – you are plain jealous because Shekhar chose me over you."

"Oh you would kill me with your jokes someday sweets." She says laughing. "And you really think I would go after someone as shallow as Shekhar? I have known him for years and I know he is a complete swine. Everyone is not as blind as you honey."

"…Oh yeah? But… why would I believe you? What proof do you have?"

"Ok, you asked for it."

She takes out her flashy expensive cell phone, press a few keys and hands it over to me.

"Here, see this video clip. And the audio is also quite clear. You can hear what they are saying."

Amit – someone tries to fix him up with someone.

It is indeed a grand party….. grander than what I can ever imagine Rishi's wedding to be. And the decorations! I mean the lights and the flowers…it is like a set created for some Ekta Kapoor's TV serials. There are endless rows of food stalls… snacks, main course and desserts of I don't know how many kinds. So many cuisines! It makes me really ponder that how many different types of people and discovered how many different types of foods and how they have different ways to peel, cut and heat them. The thought of food makes me salivate so I head towards the first stall….and its offering of pao bhaji.

"Good morning sir." I hear a kid say. Hmm, some things never change. It was the same when I was a kid it's always morning for children, no matter if its day or night. So innocent they are. I turn around and see Rohit standing with a plate in his hand.

"Hey! Rohit! Good evening. How are you?"

"I am fine sir." He says

"So *pao bhaji*?" I say looking at his plate, "nice choice I must say."
He gives me a blank look.

"Amit. How are you? I am so glad to see you here." It's Mr. Solanki.

"The pleasure is mine." I smile.

"Rohit said he wanted to get you something to eat, did he help you?"

"That is so not true dad!" Rohit suddenly protests.

"Hey! That *pao bhaji* was for me? Thank you so much." I take the plate from Rohit's hand not knowing exactly what to do with the two plates I am holding now. "You deserve a special gift for being so hospitable. I am going to get you a gift on Monday."

No reaction. "He was saying that you are his favorite teacher." Mr. Solanki says.

"Don't lie Dad." Rohit says but his red cheeks give him away. "Really? Thank you so much." I say, "And why didn't you tell me before? I always thought that you hated me. How would someone get to know if you never tell?" I hope he is able to get what I am saying. "Now I am going to get two gifts for you on Monday. One for being so hospitable, and the other for expressing your feelings." Ok, enough for the day. I don't want to make him feel more awkward.

"Amit, there is someone I want you to meet." Mr. Solanki says as he takes a plate from my hand, "Please come."

"Sure." I follow him.

I follow him till he reaches a group of people who are chatting and laughing. I wait as he approaches a pretty lady dressed in a glittering light blue saree. She listens to him, nods, and they both come together to me.

"Mr. Trehan, I want you to meet my niece, Devika."

Rimy – Will she kiss Shekhar ???

"Nice restaurant." I say. Shekhar has brought me to this impressive Thai restaurant where we have placed the order.

He looks at me and smiles, "It's my favorite."

"So who do you think is going to win?" I ask him.

"Are you kidding me? I am the clear winner here." he says as he flashes his usual smile. How strange it feels now that something I used to find incredibly charming had begun to look atrocious.

"Ha ha! No, no, I was just joking. I think we have quite a few deserving people here. I think you are very talented. And so is Kamal. Even Natasha is very good with what she does." He says.

"Hmm. Funny you didn't mention Ravi. He is your best friend." I ask him. We are sitting on a couch against the wall with the table in front of us.

He smiles again and looks at the table, tilts his head to one side and says, "Well, yes he is a very good friend of mine. But when it comes to singing and dancing, everything he knows is what I have taught him. And I feel he still has a lot to improve – a long way to go."

Wow! What a wonderful friend….bet Ravi does not know this side of Shekhar's – the way he talks about him.

There is silence for about five seconds as I really don't know what to say next. He scoots towards me and holds my hand. "But if you really ask me, I think you should win. Not only because you are the most talented person here, but because you are the most beautiful contestant as well." he keeps coming closer and closer; his lips so close to my neck that I can feel his breath against my skin.

I turn around and deliver a shy smile. "Shekhar, do you know who you look like?" I ask.

"No." he says as he starts to kiss my neck. "And its the third time—"

"YOU LOOK LIKE THE PIG WHO LIVES IN THE SLUMS BEHIND THE COLONY WHERE I STAY!" I get up and shout. He looks at me shell-shocked.

"What happened Rimz?… calm down…" he stammers.

"CALM DOWN? DO YOU REALLY EXPECT ME TO CALM DOWN AFTER SEEING THIS MISTER DOWN-ROTTEN-PATHETIC-GREATEST-CERTIFIED-RASCAL-OF-ALL-TIMES?!!!" I flip out my phone and show him the video I had copied from Natasha's mobile.

He sits there speechless.

"You know something. All Those people those four hundred years back were actually monkeys and had no idea about anything *at* all."

He looks back at me sitting there, looking like a monkey himself who is completely confused and scared.

"What do you mean?" He asks.

"Nothing." I snap. Clearly he is not well read. How would he know I am talking about Shakespear and the lines from "The Tempest".

"And take care not to come near me. EVER! Or you are going to be very very sorry. Remember we are all on a reality show which is being telecast practically all over the world." I continue.

I just say this and storm out of the restaurant like a killer heroine (to be more precise, Cameron Diaz in *Charlie's Angles*.)

Amit – Will Devika and Amit end up being together and spend the rest of their lives happily ever after?

Ok, so Devika is pretty. She is tall, with a model-like figure, curly hair, and big black eyes and very sophisticated. And like every other girl, she is also revealing a fair amount of her back. Mr. Solanki has left both of us alone.

"So Amit, Mamu says that you are a psychiatrist in Rohit's school. It's a shame that doctors are needed in school these days, no?" she says as she brushes her gorgeous hair to one side.

Oh no no! She does not know. I have to explain.

I give her a very composed smile and say, "Actually, I am not a psychiatrist, and I am a physiologist. I am a physiologist. I just help children to cope with the changes as they grow."

"Ok. So how many years have you been doing this?" she asks.

Hmm, I like that. Direct and clear. No beating about the bush. "Actually, it's not been much time... I ...worked for a real estate firm before. I was trained to be a town planner. It's just been a few weeks since I took up this job in this school." I say

"Interesting. Multifaceted guy."

I smile. "Not really. Actually you can say a stuck up guy with no where else to go."

"And humble too. I like that."

Silence.

"So?" she says

"So?" I say

"So, aren't you going to ask me anything?" she says.

"Yes… actually I was just going to ask you… what do you do?" I stammer.

"Nothing."

"Really? That is so cool!"

She smiles. "Do you mind if we go and sit there?" she says pointing towards two swings at a distance in the garden.

"Sure! Why not?"

We sit there and she starts to swing herself.

"So Amit, what is it that you want to do the most in life?" she asks.

I couldn't come up with an answer, "I guess I am a pretty content person. I can't think of anything that I really, *really* want."

"Oh! So you have a girlfriend."

"No!" I laugh, "What makes you think that?"

"You know, there is nothing more you want in life. Sounds like all is settled."

"Hmm, that is not true."

"Ok, let me put it this way. What is it that you are most passionate about?" she asks.

"Hmm, if you would ask my office colleagues, they would say that I am most passionate about environmental concerns."

"Oh God! You really don't get it do you?"

"*What?*"

"That my Mamu is up to some match making here." "Oh come on! Don't tell me that you have not sensed it." She says.

"Sensed what?"

"Matrimonial prospects! Why do you think we have been introduced the way we have been? It's really obvious Amit."

… Really? Was it?

"Really?" I try laughing, "I had no idea."

Hmm, it does make sense now come to think about it. I mean just the way Mr. Solanki introduced us both and left us *alone* in a *party*. And you know, it can be good. As Rishi says, she doesn't want to get married alone. So if this thing works, maybe we can plan a joint wedding. That will be so cool! And I won't even miss her when she is away on her honeymoon. I will be busy with mine.

Devika keeps looking at me, "You are an interesting person Amit. But I am sorry to break your heart. I am going around with someone. And there is time before I tell my family that. So I am just playing along for some time."

"Oh!"

"And you sure you don't have a girlfriend?"

"Yeah, I mean … no… I am actually between girlfriends." I stammer.

"Ok… you sound like a pro."

"No, actually I recently found out that my last girlfriend was cheating on me, so…"

"Yeah, you look like someone whose girlfriend would cheat on him." she says scrutinizing me carefully. And before I could comprehend my feelings about what she had just said, she shot the next question,

"So, tell me about your environmental concerns."

"Well these days I am working to save a piece of land that is home for a particular kind of migratory birds that come there all the way from Russia. You must have read the series of articles being featured in the newspapers these days."

Rimz – She isn't that flaky after all. Is she?

I just can't stop laughing as I tell Natasha what has happened at the restaurant.

"Oh my God. He looked like an ostrich whose eggs had just got stolen." I am in splits. I returned late and by then, dinner had finished. So I went back to the cottage only to order food from outside. And Natasha is so interested in the events of the day. We both sit there laughing our guts out.

"Oh he *so* deserved this." She says.

There is a moment of awkward silence. Then I speak up,

"You know Natasha; I always thought that you hated me. …And that was the reason why I was also not very fond of you."

"Oh shut up! You disliked me not because you felt that I hated you or anything, you disliked me because you always saw me as a potential threat to your victory in this contest."

"Yeah, it is actually true." I say meekly. "But you also never liked me."

"That is not true. I never *hated* you. It's just that… you are not someone who I would hang out with. Although you are arrogant, snooty and completely clueless about yourself and everything around you, you still have something nice about you that makes you kind of … interesting, but it's just that … I don't hang out with people like you." she shruggs as she looks at me.

"Oh, so that is why you helped me."

"No, I helped you because I hate seeing a woman losing her dignity."

Hello everyone and welcome to India's biggest talent hunt. Tonight's show is a very special one. As we are going to take you behind the cameras and into the rehearsal rooms! We went to each and every contestant and asked – who is the most undeserving contestant. And this is what they had to say.

Rimz – *"I think it's Shekhar. He is a wonderful singer but I feel that when it comes to dancing, he is not able to explore different dance forms. He is … becoming very… monotonous."*

Kamal – *"Anyone who is present here is proof enough that he/she is deserving enough to be here. Or else they wouldn't have been here."*

Ravi – *"I think it's Shekhar. Because I see… others around, who I think are better than him."*

Natasha – *"I think it's Shekhar. Because his intentions are neither pure nor singular.*

(The audience gasps)

Shekhar –"I would say it's Kamal. He seems to have a handicap when it comes to international dancing styles. I think we should look beyond his 'sweet smile and cute nose, which all the girls seem to love."

Yes, the results are shocking. Three out of our fantastic five voted Shekhar as the most undeserving contestant. And when we asked Shekhar how he felt about it, this is what he said –

"I think we all should wait and see the results. Because the best of the lot is going to win. The undeserving, will realize this, when they see the winner."

He looks extremely hurt on knowing that his best friend has voted against him. And on being asked how he felt about it, this is what he said,

"Well I understand that this is a competition and we are not friends here, but competitors."

(audience sighs)

And that's not all my dear friend. We also did an online poll to find out who was the sweetheart of every heart. And the results say...

YES! RIMZ! Can I call upon the stage our very own, very lovable RIMZ!

(Loud applause)

Rimz – The clash with the wedding (Oh no!)

I can't stop screaming and jumping with happiness as everyone comes and congratulates me. And I see Shekhar moving from one corner of the room to the other, like a monkey whose tail is on fire, talking on the phone with a very ugly, angry expression.

But there is just one teeny weeny problem. They have just announced the date of the grand finale and it is clashing with Rishika's wedding. If I tell her that, she will kill me. But I need to tell her! I must. I quickly pull out my cell phone and dial her number.

"Rimz! Hi! How are you? How is it going?" she sounds so happy. And I am going to break her heart. "I was just declared the highest voted contestant." I say.

"Great! Congrats!"

"So how are things? How're the wedding preparations?"

"Oh its fine. It's on. The usual stuff." she says.

"Rishika, there has been a little problem." I stammer.

"Why? What happened?"

"I… really feel terrible about it, but it seems that I won't be able to make it to your wedding."

"Hey! What you saying?"

"Yeah. They just announced the date for the grand finale and it's clashing with your wedding."

"Hmm, It's ok. I understand. It's once in a lifetime chance. And if not the wedding then you can always come for the reception party, right?"

"Oh yes, no questions about it."

"Cool. Even otherwise what's so special about it? It's just another wedding." She says. And she does not sound very excited.

Rimz – Shekhar is pure evil. And now she so wants to defeat him in the competition.

Ok! So we are all done with our performances for the day and the judges have also given us their comments. And now, it's time for the elimination round. I know for sure that it's going to be Shekhar. Not only because everyone hates him and he performed terribly, but also because I was successful in casting a spell of misfortune on him yesterday. Yes, I cast a spell on him. And yes, I am a witch! Oh come on, please don't act surprised as if you didn't know it. I mean, yes I am not a permanent witch, but I can be one whenever I want to be. Oh! The judges have handed over the envelope to the show host (some little known TV star) and he is going to announce the name now.

"The judges have made their decision. Tonight, one of our contestants would have to bid goodbye to this stage." The show host says.

Oh my God can't he just say it already and stop wasting our time? We all know who it is.

"And with a very heavy heart, I have to say," he carries on, "it's, Natasha." he sighs.

"NOOOOOO!!!!" I scream. I don't even know why I did that. It is like an involuntary action. Everyone turns around to stare at me instead of looking at Natasha. Oh my God what have I done? Oh my God I am so embarrassed, my cheeks are turning red. Anyway, I am sure I am not the prime focus here, and if I try hiding behind someone, I can totally get away with it. And that is what happened. Natasha is now called upon the stage, given a farewell token, a trophy and a bouquet of flowers, and then all the lights are turned off and we all sit in the dark to see the 'special moments' we have shared with Natasha.

After the shooting for the episode that is to be aired on T.V is over, I go across to Natasha.

"Hey." I say.

"Hey!" she says with a smile.

"I am really sorry that you are going. The cottage will be all empty without you."

She lets out a little laugh and says, "I am sorry that the cottage will be empty without me. But you don't have to be sorry that I am getting eliminated. This show isn't really that big a deal for me. In fact I got a call yesterday from my agent. There was a proposal for a music video and the shooting starts next week. So." She says

"Hey! That is so nice! Congratulations!"

"Thanks."

"But it was totally unexpected. You being eliminated, I mean. You have been the strongest performer till now. And I am saying that keeping all the jealousy aside." I say with a wink.

"Oh sweetheart, you still haven't got it have you?" she says

I look at her blankly.

"Honey the *show* is *rigged*!"

My blank expression continues.

"Shekhar's father is a highly respected personality and he knows the who's who of the entertainment industry."

"Oh no! Shekhar got you eliminated?" I exclaim.

She simply smiles back.

"But why? If he had any grudges it would have been against me."

"Well I am sure he must have tried that too. But the viewers love you. So that is why he could not get you out. And sweetheart, he holds a bigger grudge against me because I told you what he was up to."

"Hmm."

"And not only that. I also voted against him and said that his intentions were neither pure nor singular. I think that is what pushed him off the edge."

"He is such a *dog*!"

"Anyway, I need to go and start packing my stuff. But I must tell you that you have a very fair chance of winning this competition. If there is anyone who can beat Shekhar, it's you."

"Thanks. And I know I am going to win. Not only because I am better, but also because he does not deserve it"

"Ok, I have to go now."

"Wait! I will also come! I can help you pack!"

"So now that you are over Shekhar, who's your latest crush?" she asks as we walk towards the cottage.

"Oh no one! From now on I am going to concentrate on my performance."

"Really Rimz?" she says with a naughty smile.

"Yes Natasha."

Rimz – First impression is so not the last impression

And here we are again, Kamal and I sitting and having dinner. It's funny how untrue the saying is – first impression is the last impression.

I mean it stands untrue for everyone around me at this time. Take Shekhar, I saw him and I felt he was the best guy I had ever come across. A complete piece of crap he turned out to be. Then Kamal, I hated him when I first met him. And now he was my best friend. And Natasha, I thought I could not detest anyone more than her. It had been a full day since she had left and I still couldn't stop thinking about her.

"You really missing Natasha aren't you?" Kamal asks.

"Who me? *No!*" I deny.

"Yes you are, and you have also started lying."

How cool! I have friends who can read my mind. I can't help smiling shyly. Oh I love it when I get these expressions!

"How did you know?" I ask.

"It's written all over your face." He says, "Plus, I can't find any other logical explanation for you holding a spoonful of *dal* for a full minute as you stared at that tree there."

"Amm, by the way, I forgot to tell you, we are performing together for the next round. We have to sing a duet. I gave my name with yours in the evening today." I say

"Hmm, thanks for telling me." he smiles and says.

"You are always welcome." I say .

"Ok, tell me–" I am about to ask him something when he interrupts me.

"Oh my God!"

"What?"

"There you go again with your question and answer session." He says

"Oh shut up. Now tell me what are the three things you want the most in life?"

"Hmm. Tough one. I … don't know."

"Oh come on! How can you not know that what are the three things you want the most in life?" I say

He looks at me confused, "Are you a genie?"

"Uh! You seriously don't know?" I really can't believe it.

He smiles and shakes his head as he looks at me.

"Uh! Do you know anything about yourself at all?"

"I know that I am in the process of getting to know who I am."

"Uh! You and your philosophy again." I sigh.

"Ok, tell me what are the three things *you* want the most?" he asks me

"Oh! I am very clear about it. The three things I want the most are – personal stylist, agent, and a publicist."

He keeps looking at me with a somewhat naughty smile. And then finally says, "And how did you get to know that?"

"I was watching *High School Musical 3*. And in one of the songs, *I want it all* to be precise; there was this line – in which they sing, *personal stylist, agent, and a publicist*. And there I was, sitting in the dark, in that cinema hall, looking at the screen, and thinking 'yes, this is exactly what I want.' And that is how I realized that's what I want the most."

He is still looking at me with that same stupid smile of his.

"Hmm." He says.

Amit – Life isn't that bad after all.

It's a moment of triumph! I have done it. Well, I may not have done it yet….but it has happened. They have declared it in the newspapers. It says that the series of articles (about the environmental concerns), has won some international journalism award. THEY HAVE PUT A BAN ON ANY MORE CONSTRUCTION IN THAT AREA!!!!! Can you beat that? So much for that stupid *Shob* and that … piggy boss! Now they can both throw their heads back and deliver as many pretentious laughs as they wish. Huh! And you know what? They have also mentioned my name in the newspaper as an '*active environmentalist*'!

It is indeed a good day. I enter office, settle down and start going through my daily report to see if I have an appointment with any student today. Just then Ramesh knocks and enters the room.

"Good morning Ramesh. How are you today?"

"Fine sir. There is a letter for you."

"Oh!"

He comes and keeps the envelope on the table.

"Thank you." I say

"Thank you sir." He says and leaves.

I open the envelope,

Dear Amit,

I was delighted to see your name in today's newspaper. I didn't know you had such strong environmental concerns till Devika told me. I was really glad to see a man of strong values in today's world.

I am preparing a proposal on your behalf to protect the land and preserve it. I have already instructed a team of ecologists to ready a set of guidelines and parameters regarding managing and supervising the land. If all goes well, we should get a handsome grant from the government to create a good setup to run the 'mini bird sanctuary', which you would be managing.

I hope this works out.

Best wishes,
Amar Solanki

Rimz – A silly love song

I AM LATE!!!! I am supposed to meet Kamal at 7 near the lamp post in the garden next to the stadium AND ITS ALREADY 7:30!!!!! It is also dark. I could not help the delay. I had to decide what song we are going to perform and do the whole choreography myself. I tell you men are so lazy that they just don't do anything! Oh no! He is already there, standing next to the lamppost. I tell you, both look just the same – the lamppost and Kamal.

"I am so sorry," I say panting, "but I had to decide what we would be performing to and everything that–"

"It's ok. Chill. Relax." He says.

"Ok!" I take a deep breath and say, "We are going to sing Madonna's *I remember* – the theme song from *With Honors*. We will split the song and make a duet. It's really innovative and I am a hundred percent sure that everyone will simply love it."

"All right, all right. Here, have some water." He hands me his water bottle. "I have also prepared something. Let me give you a little demo and then we can decide which way to go."

It is dark now and the moon is rising in the horizon. There is a light breeze swaying the leaves of the trees around. He takes out an old fashioned golf cap from his bag, puts it on, and then moves to the lamp post, jumps up on the pedestal and holding the pole with one hand begins to sing,

You'd think that people would have had enough of silly love songs.
But I look around me and I see it isn't so.

He sings as he swings around the post.
Some people wanna fill the world with silly love songs.

He jumps off the pedestal and comes close to me and continues singing.

And what's wrong with thaaaaat?
I'd like to knooooow, cause here I goooo, agaaaaain,
I loooooooove yooooooou, I loooooove yoooooooou,

He holds me by my hand and turns me around.

I can't explain the feelings plain to me, say can't you see?
Ah, she gave me more, she gave it all to me
Now can't you see,

What's wrong with that
I need to know, cause here I go agaaaaaaaaaaaaain
I loooooooove yooooou, I looooove yooooou

He is not bad at all. Look at all that dancing and jumping…not to forget the song. I *like* this song! There really are other good singers too (other than Madonna). God! How did I miss out on all these things?

Love doesn't come in a minute,
Sometimes it doesn't come at all,
I only know that when I'm in it,
It isn't silly, no, it isn't silly, love isn't silly at allllllllll.

A final spin and he lands on his knee in front of me with his arms wide open. I can't avoid the grin nor can I resist clapping.

"WOW!!! That was great. We must do this. But… where is the girl's part?" I ask a little confused. He gets up panting. With a smile he says, "We will split the lyrics."

"Hmm, interesting, I like that."

"And the dance moves….for this I want you to watch 'Singing in the rain'. That is the style we wish to follow."

"Great! I am totally for this." I say, "So tell me, how you got the idea of performing this song?"

He is still gasping from all the jumping and hopping. Tiny beads of sweat have formed on his forehead and around the side burns. And another drop is rolling from the edge of his eyebrow, which make my eyes meet his. And it is actually the first time I am noticing his eyes. They are a very deep shade of brown and rather deeply set in the sockets. They are somewhat narrow and make you feel they are looking really deep inside you. And his skin is dark, but very smooth.

"I have had a childhood fascination for this song." He says panting.

"Great! Here have some water." I hand his sipper back to him.

"Thanks."

"Come, sit. Relax for a while."

"Yeah." He agrees.

"So tell me–"

"Oh God!"

"Shut up! And tell me, what kind of girl would you like? I mean … what is your type?"

And again he smiles. Oh God! Can he ever do anything more than that?

"I don't know."

"What! Do you know anything?" this guy can be really irritating at times.

"I don't know because I have not met her yet."

"God! Can someone be more lost in life?" I say.

"But I know one thing. That it has to rain the day I propose to her." He says looking upwards, as if seeing something that I am completely unable to. "And I will confess my love for her in the rain." He says as he smiles (as always).

"Hmm, and people say *I* am whimsical. Anyway, but tell me one thing, how does one get to know that it is like … true love. I mean

… how can _you_ be sure that you are not … falling for the wrong person?" I ask.

He turns around and looks at me. "Your problem is that you are searching too desperately for it. You are almost panicking. You are not able to see things clearly. You are driven too much by the physical aspect of romance; you are still to understand the difference between having sex and making love."

"Really? And what is the difference?" I ask him.

"Making out, as many people term it; is not just a physical need of the body. That is just a desire, which I believe should be controlled. If one does not control it, one would just end up having … meaningless … raw…sex. But when one is actually, truly in love, with all his heart, the act of making love is not merely a bodily need. It is an expression of the love and the emotion he has for his lover. They don't make love because their bodies demand sex; they make love because their hearts desire a deeper connection. It comes out of love and not lust. There is a difference. I hope you are getting what I am saying."

"Ha ha. Sounds like you have a lot of experience."

He again smiles and looks at me.

"O come on!" I say "Please don't tell me that you have all these notions about something that you have never experienced. I really don't believe that you have never done it."

"Well, you may or may not believe, but that won't change the truth."

"You are lying."

He smiles again.

"Then how can you claim to know what its like and what it is all about?"

He looks at me with a smile and says, "I just know."

We have all finished our performances. And all of them have been pretty good. Especially ours. People just can't stop clapping. Even the judges love it. Ranisha officially declares herself to be Kamal's fan. Even Naved sir doesn't say anything mean to me. And as always, Mannu sir cannot help his urge to flirt, "Rimz I am in love with you." He says. And I am able to pull off a very believable o-my-God-look-at-me-I-am-blushing expression. Anyway, it is elimination time once again. The envelope is here. They are going to announce the name now.

"I am really sorry to announce," The show host dressed in his shiny red suit says, "that, the one contestant who will leave us tonight is Ravi."

Uh! Good for him. It is better that he goes out this way than after losing to me in the finals. Oh! But wait a minute! That means...

"Kamal!" I exclaim. He is sitting next to me. "This means that it will be me compleating against you in the finals! As it is the judges have not liked Shekhar's performance today, so he will definitely be eliminated in the next round. Oh! Can't we both win?"

"Hmm." And that was all he says.

Amit – The bird land saved. Hurrah!!!

Hah! Today will go down as one of the best days in my life. I have not only been successful in saving the land but also probably have been able to pull off management of a full '*mini bird sanctuary*'! Yes! Today, I really want to go through my to-do list and check all that I have completed successfully. Well ...

— ~~Get a job~~ – done
— Clean the room
— Unpack the bag
— ~~Save the birdland~~ – done
— Buy fruits
— Join gym
— Find maid to cook and clean the room
— Save money to buy an iPod

Ok, so it's 2 out of 8. Hmm. What the hell! It is a great achievement and no one can deny that. Hey! I haven't spoken with Rishi in the last two days and she is getting married this Sunday. I grab my phone and dial her number.

"Hi!" I say all pepped up.

"Hi." She replies.

Ok, she sounds dull.

"So, how's everything? How are the preparations coming along?"

"It's ok. It's fine. It's ... going on." she sighs

"Rishi. *It's ok.* Everyone gets married one day. And you are going to be very happy with Iman. He is a very nice person. He is going to make you very happy."

"Amit, you should keep quiet. You are the worst judge of people! You didn't know that Sehar was cheating on you till you saw her in bed with someone else."

"That… might have … happened."

"Yes, exactly my point."

Silence.

"Rishi look, they say everyone gets cold feet on their wedding eve."

"Huh? Who *are* they?"

Hmm, yeah actually, who are the *they* in question? Members of some secret organization like it is in the Da Vinci Code? Hmm.

"Amit! Are you even paying attention to what I am saying?"

"Yes… I am completely paying attention to you." Ah! Must focus! MUST FOCUS!!!!! "I need to know how you actually feel." I just remember watching a film in which a shrink keeps asking a young boy the same question repeatedly. And it actually helps in the end. It may well be that I need to do the same with Rishi.

"I just feel… it's very unsettling. Yes, I feel unsettled."

"Hmm, unsettled is it?"

"Yes, unsettled in my professional life and unsettled in my personal life."

"Ok, about the professional life, I understand your worries. And for that I will say that it's a phase. You have to trust me for that."

"It's a phase! Amit I have been tearing my hair out trying to find an appropriate ending for my novel and it's a big round zero that I can think of!"

"Rishi, Rishi, Rishi! It's ok. It's called a writer's block. It's totally normal. Haven't you seen *Shakespeare in Love*? He felt the same way before he wrote *Romeo and Juliet* – the best play ever written. You have to take a break! Now tell me, why is it that you are feeling unsettled in your personal life?"

"I don't know! It just doesn't … feel right! It's not… coming from inside… I … can't express Amit; it's just that he has been so… imposing and insensitive lately. He wants everything his way! It's like … I don't know. I just feel that he has turned into a different person since the day I told him that we should get married."

"Rishi, if you really ask me, you are just worrying too much. You both love each other. And when you truly love someone, all such problems vanish. And … everything settles. Don't you remember how happy you were when you first started going out with him? You used to … glow with happiness! You just need to remind yourself that."

Silence.

"But Rishi, if you really feel very strongly about not marrying him, then you shouldn't."

Rima – she is very upset.

"Oh come on now, don't get upset." Kamal tries to console me.

"But … it's so unfair. You are so much better than Shekhar." I say. I know I am about to cry.

"Its ok Rima, Life doesn't end here."

"But… you are my only friend here." Ok, I can't help it anymore. Tears are rolling down my cheeks. I am officially crying.

"And that I am always going to be."

"But… Shekhar is the one who should have been eliminated! Not you!"

"Oh come on now. Stop being a baby about it." he says as he holds my face in both his hands and wipes off my tears with his thumbs.

"Come on now, smile. You don't want me to remember you like this as the-last-time-I-saw-you image do you?"

I struggle to smile but more tears come streaming down.

"Oh Kamal I am so sorry!" I break out.

"What for?" he asks surprised.

"I was very mean to you." And I remember all the times when I had treated him like dirt when we initially met.

I hug him tight as I start crying even harder.

"Rima it's ok! I never did take all that seriously."

"But they eliminated you from the contest!"

He smiles and looks directly into my eyes, "It's not a big deal." He says. "And you know what?" he continues to look at me, "You look very cute when you cry."

"Shut up" I shoot back, as I wipe my tears and struggle to kill my laughter.

Amit – It's the wedding day!!!

Rishi's d day has finally arrived. And we have two reasons to celebrate – one, Rishi is getting married and two, Rimz's making it to the finals of the talent hunt show. I am quite sure she will win. I have seen Shekhar in a few episodes and he seems such a loser. Our Rimz rocks!

Everything is in place at the venue of the wedding. Even Rishi has returned from the beauty parlor on time. No delays whatsoever. All the family and friends are here. The hall looks regal but it is raining cats and dogs outside. It's been so for the past 3 days now. So there I am mingling with the guests and checking on the food being served. Oh! What am I saying? Rishi and I had decided the menu after all. I turn to the stall serving the *aloo tikki*. It's been such a long time since I had eaten one. With all those chutneys and everything…. Hmm, yum yum yum.

Just then I see the event manager heading towards me. What is it? Have I done something wrong? Are hosts of a party not entitled to eat?

"Sir, Madam is calling you to her room." He says.

"Oh! Is it?" I say.

"Yes sir."

"Everything is alright up there, right?" I look at him and ask as a feel a pull of anxiety.

"Yes sir, everything is just fine. All the arrangements are in place."

Uh! I mean to ask if everything is fine with Rishi! Duffer!

"Good." I say and turn around and march towards Rishi's room.

I stand outside the door and knock.

"Come in." Rishi says from inside.

I enter the room and am stunned to see Rishi sitting in front of the dressing table. It feels like a scene straight out of Kuch Kuch Hota Hai when Shah Rukh enters Kajol's room. I smile, "You are looking very beautiful. I hope you have got yourself clicked. Because after the wedding you are going to look tired and … "

She is looking at me with a blank expression.

"What's wrong Rishi?" I ask.

"Iman is cheating on me."

"WHAT? Please don't start with all that again–"

"The report from that private detective just came in."

"WHAT? You actually hired a–"

Before I finish my sentence she takes out a few photographs and puts them in front of me on the table.

"Oh no!" I say. There are four pictures in total. Iman is with the same girl in all four of them. In the first one, they are sitting in some restaurant and he is holding her hand. It seems they are all set to have a candle light dinner. In another, he is sitting with her on a bench in a park and has a hand around her waist and is kissing her neck. In another they are walking holding hands in a market place. And in the fourth Iman is driving a car and that slutty girl is resting her head on his shoulder. Oh no!!

"But wait a minute, how do we know that these pictures are … genuine and not … morphed?" I ask.

"Amit! Don't you dare try proving to me that he is innocent."

"…Ok…" I finally give in. "And you know what? I always have my doubts like this, I have this way of being overly optimistic at times, and maybe that is why I was never able to figure out that Sehar was cheating on me."

"Amit. I don't want to marry him."

"It's ok Rishi. Even I don't think …"

"I think I want to run away from the wedding."

"What! Are you out of your mind? We should wait for the *baraat*, talk it out with Iman, tell him that we know everything now, and then see how things take shape."

"Oh please Amit! I am not going to do that. Huh! I would be better off marrying you than him."

"Oh no!" I crash on a chair. "So it's actually turning out to be just like they show in the movies. You are going to elope with me on your wedding day, and we are going to get married somewhere in the mountains. …"

"Oh shut up! We are not getting married or anything even remotely close to that. You are just helping me run away from this place."

"Oh! But Rishi… you just can't run away from your wedding like this. I…. I agree it's not good to marry a guy who is cheating on you but…"

"Yes I can. And you are going to help me do that. We have to run away."

"But… how are we going do that?" I ask.

"I don't know! Where are my car keys? We have to run away." She repeats.

"It's raining outside!" I look outside the window into the dark night. A huge bolt of lightning is followed by a loud roar of thunder.

"Yes we would get wet! Big deal."

"But..."

"Amit what's the matter with you! Why are you always such a ... chicken?"

"But... you are wearing your ... fifty kg wedding dress."

"I KNOW THAT. WHERE THE HELL ARE THE KEYS?"

"How are we going to... go? It's raining!"

"I know! And you are the most useless man I have ever come across. You are supposed to drive me away and here I am, driving myself and you! THE KEYS! I FOUND THE KEYS!"

"But ..."

"JUST SHUT UP AND RUN!"

Rimz – The final victory.

The past three days have been hellish. Not only has it been raining in Kolkata, but I am also missing my best friend's wedding. I am preparing for the finals of the dance competition on my own and I am just not used to rehearsing without Kamal. But anyway, what will be, will be. And the way it rains here! My God! I have never seen such a downpour! It is more an infinite waterfall from the skies than the rains. But thankfully, right now it's only drizzling.

My d day dawns. I am missing Kamal more than ever. I didn't know why but I have always imagined myself running to him and hugging him and shouting and screaming once I have won the contest. Anyway, now I have to focus. I am going to perform the best song ever written – Madonna's Erotica. And I have been practicing very hard.

Shekhar has just performed and all the girls in the audience are literally going crazy screaming his name 'Shekhaaaaaar we looooove youuuuuu.' God! How can people be so dumb and disillusionalized?

"And now we call upon stage our other finalist to mesmerize us with one more dazzling performance," announces the show host. I have been seeing this guy on this stage for the past two months now and I feel a little stupid for still not knowing his name.

I get up, sorely missing Kamal who is not there to wish me luck. I walk to the stage and stand right at the center. The lights blind me and I can hardly see anyone for a moment. But this is the place I have always dreamed of, the moment I have always wished for myself. My dream is about to be fulfilled. But I can't feel anything. I can hear the audience cheering for me. But it creates no rush. I close my eyes and gather all my courage to say what I want to. And as I close my eyes, I see Kamal's smiling face once again. I open my eyes and look for Kamal, wondering all the while if he is here in the audience today. But the lights are too bright and I can't see a single face.

Suddenly I don't feel like performing Erotica.

"Tonight's song, ladies and gentlemen, I dedicate to my very dear friend Kamal. It was his… dream to sing this for the finals. But… he was not able to make it. Kamal, this is for you."

The audience applauds and cheers.

I go and inform the musicians about the change in plan, and which song they should play. I somehow know that Kamal would be watching the show being aired on T.V somewhere. And I went to do something for him.

The music starts. And I sing,

> *You know I can't smile without you*
> *I can't smile without you*
> *I can't laugh and I can't sing*
> *I'm finding it hard to do anything*

I have spent some great moments with him. And I … don't even have a picture of his. And I am so sure he is not on any of the social networking sites neither Facebook, nor Orkut! God! I feel so much like Kate Winslet from Titanic! sob! sob!

> *You see I feel sad when you're sad*
> *I feel glad when you're glad*

If you only knew what I'm going through
I just can't smile without you

He has helped me so many times. He has taught me so many things.
If only I knew what you meant to me when you were around. I
remember how much fun we had having those *bhindies* together.

You came along just like a song
And brightened my day
Who would have believed that you were part of a dream
Now it all seems light years away...

I sing these lines and I just can't control myself anymore. My
voice cracks and endless tears stream down my cheeks. He used to
gaze at the stars light years away. This is not what I want. This is
not where I want to be! I want him! I want to be with him! I
want to tell him that being called sexy sena is not my darkest
secret. It is that I liked *Jhoom Barabar Jhoom* and *Tashan*! And
now there is no way to find him and tell him so. It is too late. I
can't sing anymore and I stop. I stare blankly at the audience and
blurt, "I am sorry." I say and I run off the stage. I go out of the
hall. It's still drizzling outside. There is only one place that I feel
like going to at this moment...and it is to the park next to the
stadium. I want to sit by the lamppost and remember the time
when we rehearsed there. Tomorrow I will have to leave all this
and go back. I want to strengthen and relive the memories once
before I leave.

I enter the park, go to the lamppost and sit down next to it. There
is a streak of lightning and loud thunder. It is starting to rain harder.
I want to see the stars tonight and feel all that Kamal had felt when

he had seen them. I feel desperate and lonely and I can't spot the stars tonight.

> *You came along just like a song*
> *And brightened my day*
> *Who would have believed that you were part of a dream*
> *Now it all seems light years away*

Great! Now I am hearing voices.

> *And now you know I can't smile without you*
> *I can't smile without you*
> *I can't laugh and I can't sing*
> *I'm finding it hard to do anything*

The voice continues and I look up. A shadow emerges from behind. The lamp post around which Kamal danced once.

> *You see I feel sad when you're sad*
> *I feel glad when you're glad*
> *If you only knew what I'm going through*
> *I just can't smile*

He continues to sing and he walks towards me in the rain. I experience a thrill as I had never experienced before. It is Kamal. And he is here.

"KAMAL!" I scream as I run to him and hug him. "I missed you. I missed you so much."

"I missed you too." he says smiling at me.

Now some people say happiness takes so very long to find
Well, I'm finding it hard leaving your love behind me

And you see I can't smile without you
I can't smile without you
I can't laugh …

Nobody is singing these lines now. It's the narrator back again. He takes on from here. I am busy now. I have a lot to tell Kamal (but not the darkest secret of all. That, I will keep for another time.) Anyway, you guys have fun. I am off for now ☺

"It's raining," Rima says as she walks holding his hand, resting her head on his shoulder.

"I know," says Kamal.

And after that...

What happened after that? Well, Rishika finally found an ending for her novel. The protagonist of her story realized that unlike a typical Indian girl, she does not want to live the false dream of finding a 'soul mate' and settling down with him, spending the rest of her life making compromises every bit of the way. She realized that she is a free bird and wants to stay that way. (Life is perhaps just not the way they show in the movies, after all.) She sent the manuscript to the publisher again and this time they loved it. Her book is scheduled to hit the stands next month.

Rima started a fashion consultancy firm in Delhi after returning from Kolkata. She is really happy running the firm and is doing very well. (She still does not accept that disillusionalized is no word.)

Kamal got an offer from a music company and signed a 3 year contract with them. He is also in Delhi now.

Mr Solanki managed to get Amit's proposal approved, and got a huge grant for him. He assisted him in developing a system to manage the mini bird sanctuary. Amit kept a tiny part of the grant for himself. Now his 'to do' list reads like this —

— ~~Get a job~~ – done
— ~~Clean the room~~ – done
— ~~Unpack the bag~~ – done
— ~~Save the birdland~~ – double done
— ~~Buy fruits~~ – done
— ~~Join gym~~ (given up)
— ~~Find maid to cook and clean the room~~ – done

— ~~Save money to buy an ipod~~ – done

And by the way, Amit has a name for the bird sanctuary. It is 'The Bird land'.

Its time again – thank you!

Here we go again. Another story has come to an end and its time again to thank everyone who helped me write 'Just Like In The Movies'.

As always, I would like to start by saying that a book is never written by the writer alone. It is written by him, and everyone around him be it directly or indirectly. So, I would like to thank my family – my Mom, Dad, my sister Anu, Chote Daddy, Chote Mom – thank you for everything. And Brutus, you may not be physically present with me anymore, but god knows, the love I have for you would always remain – you were my only friend all through my growing years

A Big thanks to everyone at Srishti – all of this, I owe to you. None of this would have been possible if you would not have believed in my work. And I am not saying it just like that – I really mean it from the bottom of my heart.

Writer's Side – I can't thank you guys enough. You did a terrific job. Thank you so much!

Novoneel – thank you so much for helping me out with the blurb. You know how desperately stuck I was that time.

Bhaskar – for all the help and support, I really cant thank you enough.

Kunal, you not only read the whole manuscript, but also helped me with all the rephrasing. Thank you.

Sumit Kumar – Thank you for your valuable comments (and time).

Shilpa, Shweta, Prateek and Nitika – thank you so much for being around and help me write.

Guneet, Rinku, Shipra, Aksha, Pragya, Ayodh, Swati, Shivani, Vinayak, Benny, Anuja, Shalini, Saumya and all the others – Thank you. (I am really sorry if I have missed someone out, but you all know how important you are for me.)

Dolly Raj Singh Aunty – thank you so much for the cakes, the yummy meals, and all the words of encouragement. You always make me feel that I can make it big.

Naveen Baiya, Sheena didi, Bhavya and Parth – thanks for all they support and all those wonderful times.

My online friends – as this list is very long and I cant possibly manage to mention everyone here. So what I am gonna say is – everyone in my Facebook and Orkut friends list – Thank you so much. You guys constitute my basic support system.

And all of my readers (Himani Goyal – you were my first reader and I remember that) – thank you. If it wasn't for you all, I would not be writing.

Thank you so much everyone!

Thank you!!!